CANYON SHOWDOWN

BARRY CORD

SAGEBRUSH
Large Print Westerns

First published in Great Britain by Hale
First published in the United States by Arcadia House

First Isis Edition
published 2019
by arrangement with
Golden West Literary Agency

A catalogue record for this book is available
from the British Library.

ISBN 978–1–78541–680–4 (pb)

Published by
F. A. Thorpe (Publishing)
Anstey, Leicestershire

Set by Words & Graphics Ltd.
Anstey, Leicestershire
Printed and bound in Great Britain by
T. J. International Ltd., Padstow, Cornwall

This book is printed on acid-free paper

CHAPTER
ONE

The big roan's snort of alarm warned Dave Chance. He was standing knee deep in the slow-flowing creek, rubbing some of the dust and grime of a long dry trail from himself. He turned fast, fighting the pull of the water against his thighs.

He didn't make it to the bank in time.

The man crouched in the striped shade of the drooping willows whirled at the sound of Dave's splashing. He had been going through Dave's clothing; now he spun around to face the big man, and he was holding Dave's worn Remington .44 in his pudgy hand.

The hammer made an audible click as he thumbed it back. He was a man obviously not used to guns, which made him the more dangerous. His fleshy face was drawn and sweat-streaked, and his breathing was labored, as though he had been running in the hot sun for some time.

"Stay easy, mister!" he snarled. "I'm not after your skin! I just want to borrow this gun and your horse —"

He was backing away as he talked. The willows whispered at the passing of a stray breeze, and he jerked a nervous glance toward the rock-strewn slope down which he must have come.

He's afraid of someone, Dave thought, and he's just nervous enough to use that gun at any sudden move.

So he stood still, the stream sliding just below his knees, his big hard-knuckled hands feeling useless at his sides. Morning sunlight made its broken pattern on the creek flowing through low stony hills; it reflected upward across Dave's broad, muscled chest, and his eyes seemed to light with a deep blue fire. He waited, studying the obviously harassed prowler with a look of wry humor at his own predicament.

The man backing toward Dave's horse was middle-aged, ruddy-faced and soft-bellied. A ragged brown mustache partially hid a bulbous nose which still held the small indentations made by steel-rimmed spectacles. But he was not wearing his spectacles now. He was dressed in soiled whipcord britches and a tan twill shirt. He was bareheaded, and where his thining brown hair had receded from his forehead, the sun had stamped its red brand.

He was moving crab-like along the bank, keeping the Remington leveled at Dave. The roan threw up its head and eyed the stranger.

"I'll leave him at Jacob's Stables in Paydirt," the man said. His voice was hurried, uncertain. He licked his lips and paused to reach in a hip pocket for a handkerchief to wipe his sweaty face. "Hate to do this to you, mister. But I need this animal more than you do right now. You'll find him in Jacob's, and I'll pay you well for the loan."

He reached the roan's side and glanced down at the saddle Chance had dropped by the base of the willows.

Discouragement spread across his soft face. He stared hard at Dave, at the saddle, and Chance could almost see his mind working, wondering how he could saddle the big roan and still keep Dave at bay.

He got the blanket over the roan's back first, talking gently to the big stallion. He managed this with one hand, but haste was pushing him, and he worked nervously.

The roan let the stranger work on him. He stood rigid, ears pricked back, eyeing Dave for the signal that would turn him into an iron-shod killer. He was a one-man animal. Dave had bought him right after the war; the roan had cost him six months' pay, earned working for the cattle-rich, money-poor, big Circle T Ranch on the Brazos. He had worked many other places and done a lot of other things since, but he had managed to keep the roan with him.

"Nice animal," the thief said sincerely. "Gentle, too." He was awkward as he lifted the saddle with one hand and tried to toss it over the roan's back. He didn't have the strength in his arm to do it.

"Better use both hands, fella," Dave advised easily.

The man flushed. But he decided to take the chance. He thrust Dave's Remington inside his waistband and heaved the saddle over the stallion's back. Then he clawed at the gun again, drawing it and swinging around to face the big man in the stream.

Dave Chance had made no move.

"Thanks," the horse thief muttered. He licked his lips again as he turned, tightened the cinches and lifted his left foot into the stirrup. The roan was like a statue, ears pricked forward, waiting for Dave to tell him what to do.

The man lifted himself into the saddle. "Look me up at the Canyon House," he called back to Dave. "I'll make this up to you. The name is Irving Ram —"

The rifle shot cut him off. The whiplash of the .30–30 explosion echoed sharply among the rocky hills bordering the narrow creek.

Irving sagged over the roan's neck. The big stallion whirled with the shot, and the man slid off, limp as a sack of meal. He fell with a sudden thud.

Dave made the bank with the shot still echoing in the hills. His naked body flashed in the sun. He made a run for the roan, who came to meet him; the second rifle shot came high, whipping through the drooping branches of the willows.

Chance jerked his rifle from the roan's saddle scabbard and slapped the animal on the rump. "Get out of sight, fella!" he snapped, and lunged ahead for the slim protection of the foot-thick willow trunk.

The shots had come from the rocky ridge a hundred yards down south of the creek, the same ridge down which Irving had come. Dave levered a shell into firing position as he hugged the tree; he was counting on the dappled pattern of shadow and sunlight to screen him from the rifleman on the ridge.

There were two of them on the slope, partially hidden by towering gray rocks which seemed to grow out of the dun-colored earth. One of them was standing tall in the stirrups of a claybank horse, sighting down

4

the barrel of his rifle. He was wearing a high-crowned gray Stetson, and his dark woolen shirt made a contrast against the dun-colored rocks. The other man, visible only for a moment, was riding for cover behind another rocky upthrust.

Dave's quick shot, ricocheting off the rock face a foot from the claybank's rider's face, startled him; he jerked as he pulled the trigger, and his bullet whipped high over Dave's head. Chance's blue eyes had a deadly glint as he figured Kentucky windage and slammed another shot up at the rifleman.

The rider twisted in the saddle, and his next shot went straight up into the air. He fell forward on the claybank's neck, his left hand clutching at the horse's long mane. Something fell from his shirt pocket, something that glinted in the sunlight. Then the claybank, at his urging, was wheeling, lunging back among the sheltering rocks.

His companion fired once, but he was guessing at Dave's position, and his shot was wide. Dave laid three fast shots among the rocks where the man's smoke showed, the slugs ricocheting and whining in the hot sunlight. The explosions bounced among the rocky hills and finally faded — and then Dave caught the faint drum of hoofs heading south, receding.

He settled back against the willow and took a deep breath, and the smile that crinkled his lips was hard and held little humor.

"Sure caught me with my pants down," he muttered. And then, remembering the horse thief who had tried to get away on his roan, he turned and walked over to him.

The man lay sprawled in the sun, just beyond the shadow of the willow. Blood made a dark, spreading stain under his left arm. His breathing was barely perceptible, but Dave saw that he was still alive.

Dave knelt beside the man. He was on his back, staring up at the hot blue sky. He became aware of Dave's presence slowly, as though he were returning from far away. His pale eyes focused with an effort.

"Get Sonner —" he said. His chest rose and his lips moved slowly, forcing his words. "Get Doc Sonner —"

Dave's eyes held a fleeting compassion. It was much too late for a doctor.

The man's breath went out in a choked gurgle. He lay still in the sun, staring up at the sky with unseeing eyes.

Dave looked him over. He studied the red welts around the man's wrists, and they suddenly made the pattern clear. Whoever he was, this man had been held prisoner somewhere, no doubt by the two riflemen who had come looking for him. Obviously he had escaped them, and judging from the sunburn on his forehead, he had been afoot and running since morning.

That much Dave guessed. But his thinking went no further — he was not directly concerned with this man, or with those who had killed him. This would be the responsibility of the local sheriff, and Dave had developed a cynical attitude about the type of law he encountered in rough mining towns.

He pulled his thoughts back to the present as the roan came, stepping deliberately, neck arched in curiosity.

Dave straightened. He stepped across Irving's body, picked up his Remington, which the man had dropped as he fell out of the saddle, and turned to the roan, who was sniffing at the body.

"He's dead, fella," Chance muttered. "Made a pretty poor horse thief. I was going to let him get settled in the saddle before giving you the word to dump him. But they beat me to it."

The roan looked toward the ridge, and Dave grinned briefly as he went back for his clothing. He dressed, buckled his worn gun belt about his hard-muscled waist and walked back to the horse standing over the body.

He was a big man, standing almost two inches over six feet, and at the moment he weighed one hundred and ninety pounds. He had eaten one decent meal in two days, and he had taken his belt in two notches. Yet he was not lean, like most of the riders who worked for cattle outfits and lived most of their active life in the saddle.

He was a solid man who moved lightly and fast; he had trained himself this way, and most of the years now behind him he had made his living, precarious as it was, as a fighter. He had toured frontier towns taking on the local bully for whatever purse the local citizens felt inclined to offer. He bore the tiny scars of his calling in healed white lines over his right eye, a silghtly bent nose, and broken knuckles set too often.

Dave Chance — fighter. It was his manager, Johnny Cruze, who had grimly nicknamed him "Last Chance," just before he had run out on him with the fighter's purse and the money he had collected betting on him.

Dave stood there by the roan, caught in bitter reflection.

He was a man who somehow had always been a step behind the big chance; the sort of man who always just missed out. In the late war, he had missed making sergeant because Lee surrendered to Grant two days before his warrant was signed. He was a shade too slow, but he had backhanded Wesley Hardin in the mouth in a barroom argument and then tried to beat the famed gunman to the draw. He carried the scar of Hardin's bullet just under his collar-bone.

Events had the habit of being over when he got there; it had brought him to the age of thirty-four, a big, powerful man with a slightly battered face.

The roan's impatient snort roused him. He picked up the Winchester he had laid down beside the dead man and reloaded the magazine with cartridges from a box he carried in his saddlebag.

He came back and shoved the rifle into its saddle scabbard. The roan shifted and then stood still as Dave lifted the dead man and slid him across the saddle.

"Let's take a look on the ridge," Dave muttered. He was used to talking to himself, the mark of a bitter, lonely man.

He rode up among the rocks where the claybank rider had stood up in his stirrups to fire. Bending sidewise in the saddle, Dave spotted the brass casings of a .30 caliber rifle, a common enough weapon in that country, and stepped down to pick them up. No unusual markings caught his eye, but he noticed drops of blood turned brown on the flat stone a few steps away, and near it he found a small mouth organ.

Dave picked it up and read the German maker's name stamped on it. He dropped the harmonica into his pocket and stepped up into the saddle again. He crested the ridge and looked back; the clear stream below looked like molten brass in the sun.

Ahead of him to the southwest the land stretched rocky and desolate, rising to meet the first granite rises of the Anvils. A narrow trail came out of the east and faded in the direction of a canyon pass in the hills.

The town of Paydirt lay in that direction; and that was where Dave Chance was headed.

CHAPTER
TWO

Devil's Creek made a booming noise in the darkness, filling the night with its presence. A chill wind slid down off the granite peaks that shone a ghostly white in the moonlight and whistled through Paydirt's narrow, twisted streets.

Down by the warehouse section, a freight was making up for its run of twenty-six twisting, tortuous miles up Devil's Canyon to the Lucky Cuss mine on the shoulder of Big Lars peak. The Mallet engine's patient hissing competed with the wind and the booming from the river, but it was neither of these sounds which brought the girl to the door of the small red brick building facing Gold Street.

The sign over the door read: "Sheriff's Office, Hidalgo County." It had been built during Paydirt's earlier boom, when the Arizona town had seemed destined to stand with Phoenix and Tucson as a growing metropolis, only to fade quickly when the strikes abruptly petered out.

Paydirt was booming again. But it was a mild boom this time. It had come at a time when the town had all but given up hope, and Paydirt's luck was darkened by a well-earned skepticism. There was no telling how long the new strike at the Lucky Cuss would keep paying off, and Paydirt would live or die on this answer.

Laura Soltight turned to face the bridge across Devil's Creek. Paydirt had grown up on this side of the canyon; the newer section across the creek had been settled after the reopening of the Lucky Cuss mine.

The wind carried the faint yells of a crowd, rising and fading in a rhythm that held bitter meaning for her. She listened, stiff and fearful, and each swell of sound shook her.

Behind her the office was empty. Her father's pipe was on his desk, the bowl still warm; and filling her thoughts was the hurting memory of her brother's white, taut face.

She didn't hear the rider who came out of the street shadows.

"Evening, ma'am," the masculine voice greeted her politely.

Laura jerked around. She reached her right hand around the door jamb for the shotgun she had placed there and brought the weapon up in a swift decisive gesture.

The rider standing just off the splash of lamplight from the office was a big man. She could make out the spread of wide shoulders tapering down to a flat, hard belly. But the face shadowed by a down-tilted Stetson was hidden from her probing glance. He was sitting in the saddle of a big roan stallion who regarded her with intelligent eyes.

There was a figure draped across the saddle in front of the man, but Laura saw only a shapeless shadow, and it meant nothing to her; she had come to feel, through bitter experience, that all strangers were hostile.

Neither man nor horse moved at the threat of the shotgun in her hands. But a dry humor colored the rider's quiet voice.

"Can you direct me to Sheriff Soltight's office, ma'am?"

Laura peered more closely at the man, trying to measure the silent figure behind the brush jacket protecting him from the bitter wind. The darkness hid his face. But she did see the holstered gun at his hip, and instinctively she tightened her grip on her shotgun.

Another one, she thought despairingly, and fear added its weight to the dismal feeling that had oppressed her. *Another killer riding into Paydirt, drawn by rumors of gold!*

"This is the sheriff's office," she answered coldly.

The tall man looked her over with detached appraisal. "My mistake," he said gently. "I thought the sheriff was a man."

She reddened. "He's my father."

"Is he in?"

She made a slight motion with the shotgun toward the plank bridge. A wild, sustained roar came to them, and she winced, feeling the cruelty that was behind the crowd's concerted outcry.

"He's across the river," she said grimly, "with my brother, Rick."

The rider glanced toward the light-splotched shadows of the newer section. Darkness hid the small frown in his eyes. "Where shall I find your father, ma'am?"

"In the Golden Nugget." A faint sneer crept unconsciously into the girl's tone. "But I wouldn't advise you to look for him in there."

The rider's smile held a bleakness she did not see. "Thank you, Miss Soltight," he murmured. He touched his hat brim as he turned the big roan aside.

Judging from the sound, most of Paydirt was concentrated in the Golden Nugget tonight.

Dave found a spot in the rack two doors past the Golden Nugget. He was curious about what was going on inside the big gambling hall, but he wanted to see the sheriff, too. The body he had brought in to Paydirt was the sheriff's responsibility, and Chance wanted to start off on the right side of the law in Paydirt.

He dismounted and left the stallion with its limp burden at the tie-rack and pushed through the crowd clustered around the gambling hall doors. The men resented his passage, but they let him through.

The Golden Nugget was big, brightly lighted by a half-dozen imitation crystal chandeliers. The first thing Dave noticed were the spangled, tight-skirted girls lining the banister of the second floor staircase. They were pressed against the mahogany railing, staring down into the middle of the big crowd, eyes gleaming with excitement.

One of them shrilled: "Kill him, Packy! Break his jaw!"

Dave shouldered a way toward the long bar. He found a place at the rail and turned to watch. Under the bright lights of the center chandelier, a fight ring had been roped off. There was only one strand connecting the four wobbly ring posts, and it sagged now under the weight of the man sprawled across it.

He was a big, strong-looking boy with cornmeal yellow hair and a cowlick coming down over his bloodied face. His features were distorted, swollen. His lips were parted in a strained, terrible grimace as he pawed with an ineffectual left hand at the bull-chested, swarthy man standing over him.

The dark-skinned fighter had a bruise high on one cheek, but otherwise he was unmarked. His taped hands flashed out, sinking with a meaty thud into the blond man's quivering side. Around the makeshift ring the yells of the motley crowd rode high.

Dave watched the ending of the obviously one-sided fight, caught by the violence of the scene. The swarthy man was slightly shorter than the helpless blond youngster on the rope, but he moved lightly, professionally, and his lips were pulled back in a feral snarl. He was smashing at the youngster's kidneys, ignoring the unprotected jaw. A solid smash now would end the brutal punishment and save what was left of the boy's pride.

But the swarthy man was not out to end the fight that quickly. He shoved the sagging figure up with his left hand and continued to pound the man's kidneys with his right; short chopping blows that twisted the boy's lips with terrible pain.

14

A thick-shouldered, grizzled man shoved spectators out of his way as he reached the youngster on the rope. He put a protective arm around the helpless boy's shoulders, and a gun glinted with grim authority in the flickering light of the chandeliers.

"All right," he snarled. "He's had enough! You want to kill him?"

The swarty fighter stood under the lights, sweat running down his muscled chest where black hair curled tightly. He clasped his hands over his head in an arrogant gesture of victory as he turned and grinned at the yelling crowd.

A small slight man in a flowered waistcoat, long tan coat and fawn-colored trousers had been watching the fight with cool detachment from the far end of the bar. A jeweled stickpin flashed as he turned and crooked a finger to one of the bartenders. The man hurried over and leaned deferentially over the counter, nodding as he stepped back.

Reaching under the counter, he brought up a wooden bung starter and pounded on the bar with it.

"Duke says the drinks are on the house!" he yelled as the crowd quieted. "Come and get it!"

There was a rush for the bar. Men crowded two and three deep around Dave, but something in the big stranger's cold gaze stopped those nearest him from crowding. They gave the tall man elbow room instinctively.

A slight, gray-templed man in a rumpled black suit joined the sheriff. Together they lifted the battered youngster off the rope and helped him under it. Draping the kid's arms over their shoulders, they started for the door.

The sheriff held his Colt in his right hand, his square jaw set, iron defiance in his gray eyes. The boy's feet dragged across the wide floor boards.

Dave watched them head for the door amid the jeers of the crowd. They were intercepted by a lean-flanked, cat-footed man in a black cotton shirt and pin-striped trousers. He was a hard-faced individual in his early twenties, and he carried a cold authority in the badge that glittered on his shirt and in the low-slung Remington .44 on his thigh, thonged down and moving like a part of him.

They conferred by the door. Dave saw Sheriff Soltight shake his head. The other shrugged and turned away, heading for the table he had left.

A few feet from Dave, two serious-faced men in town clothes were pushing money across the counter to the grinning bartender. They turned and left, joining the sheriff at the door.

The slant-eyed individual guzzling his drink next to Dave Chance chortled: "Duke shore showed up that derned uptown crowd! After the beating Packy gave the sheriff's loud-mouthed son, they won't be bothering this side of Devil's Creek in a hurry!"

"Grudge fight?" Dave asked idly.

"Yeah." The other nodded, banging on the counter with his empty glass for- a refill. "Rick Soltight kinda took a shine to one of Duke's gals, an' Packy told him to lay off. Rick sassed him, an' Duke stepped in an' suggested they settle it in the ring." He watched eagerly as the bartender slopped whiskey into his empty glass.

"Leave it to Duke to make money," he added slyly. He wiped his lips with his sleeve. "Couple of the sheriff's cronies lost a pile of dinero to Duke tonight, betting on his boy." He guzzled his drink and reached his glass out for another refill.

The bartender shook his head and raised his voice above the bar clamor. "That's all, gents! Paying customers only now!"

The drinker sidled away with a disappointed mutter. The clamor began to subside; the bar line thinned as the freeloaders drifted away. The girls came down from the staircase and began mingling with the customers.

Two of Duke's men started to take down the improvised ring. Nursing his drink, Dave saw the swarthy fighter emerge from a back room. Packy had pulled a black turtle-necked sweater over his barrel chest, and his black hair had a high pomade gloss in the lamplight.

He nodded at the calls of admiration which greeted him and came across the big room, heading for the bar. A drunk weaved across his path, and Packy jammed the heel of his palm into the man's face. The drink piled into a card table, overturned it and lay still.

Dave's eyes held a wicked expectancy. He reacted instinctively to physical arrogance, and now he felt a pulse of recklessness throb through him. He turned back to the bar and picked up his drink. It was time for him to go. He had a body to turn over to the law, and a few questions of his own to ask. Johnny Cruze was in Paydirt, but he might not be using his real name.

He heard Packy come up to the bar, a light-stepping man for all his size. But the hand that fell on Dave's shoulder was not light. It was a hard, impatient hand, and it pulled him roughly around, shoved him contemptuously aside.

Packy's voice held a gravelly insolence. "Out of my way, pilgrim! I need room when I drink!"

Temper ran like a brush fire through Dave Chance. He was a man who took no shoving, and he turned now to appraise the burly fighter bellying up to the bar.

Packy was reaching for the bottle the bartender placed in front of him. He poured himself a generous shot and started to lift the glass to his lips.

Chance coldly and deliberately jostled his arm.

Whiskey spilled down Packy's stubbled chin and onto his sweater. It dribbled and made dark stains, and for a moment the shock of Dave's action held the fighter in a sort of puzzled trance.

Then his head came around slowly on his thick neck, and his yellow-green eyes met Dave's cool blue ones. Chance was remembering the youngster who had taken a cruel and unnecessary beating at the hands of this man.

"Reckon some gents are just naturally sloppy drinkers," Dave commented thinly.

Packy's curse and movement were simultaneous. He dropped his glass and pivoted, driving his right in a vicious hook for Dave's face.

Dave moved his head four inches to one side. Packy's fist slid over his shoulder, and the force of the burly man's swing brought him around and up against Chance.

No one saw the iron-hard fist that sank wrist deep in the fighter's solar plexus. But the shock of that blow burst like a startled light in Packy's eyes; his dark face turned a muddy coffee color. His knees started to buckle.

Dave stepped back and whipped his left hand around in a solid smash to Packy's jaw.

The fighter blindly put a hand out for the counter. Then his knees buckled and he went down, sliding limply between the brass rail and the base of the bar.

CHAPTER
THREE

It had started and ended fast, and no one clearly saw what had happened. The men standing close to Packy turned, stared at the crumpled figure with startled, unbelieving eyes and began to edge away.

The bartender scowled. He placed both hands on the counter leaned over it and looked down at the unconscious fighter; then he eased back and stared at Dave, his mouth making a lopsided O.

The uneasy silence spread along the bar to Duke Mason. The owner of the Golden Nugget had his back to the bar and was sucking on an expensive Havana cigar. He felt the stir among the men near him, and one of them muttered: "What happened to Packy?"

He turned quickly, frowning, and the men backing away from the brass rail gave Duke a clear view of Packy's sprawled figure and the tall, broad-shouldered stranger standing over him.

Surprise prodded him erect, his teeth clamped down on his cigar. He started for Dave, his dark, cold gaze moving from Dave's impassive features to those of the open-mouthed bartender.

"What the devil's going on here, Sid?" he snapped. "What's happened to Packy?"

The bartender shook his head. "Don't rightly know, Duke," he mumbled. He shot a glance at Chance. "This jasper made Packy spill his drink, and Packy threw a punch at him. Next thing I knew, Packy was going down —"

The gambler turned his narrowing gave on Chance. "What did you hit him with? Brass knuckles?"

Dave shrugged. He started to turn, to finish his drink. He had not wanted to get involved here, and he regretted his temper now. But inside him he felt a cynical expectancy build up, and he knew from experience that these things were like a chain, each link hooked to another, leading only to more trouble.

He wanted to leave, but Duke would have none of it. The gambler's voice probed harshly: "Just a minute, fella! I asked you a plain question. I'm in the habit of getting answers!"

Dave turned. "Maybe your fighter has a glass jaw," he suggested.

Duke's eyes glittered with a murky light. Slow laughter bubbled from him. "You pore darn fool!" he sneered. "Packy'll kill you when he comes to!"

Dave's glance dropped to the man who was stirring, pawing dazedly at the brass rail in an effort to pull himself up to a sitting position. "Don't bet on it!" he answered shortly, and turned to leave.

He was five paces away from the bar, heading for the swinging doors. He caught Duke's blurred reflection in the window glass, whirled and fired.

He shot to kill. But his bullet was high, clipping the lobe neatly from Duke's left ear.

Duke's right hand was inside his coat, reaching for his underarm gun. He froze, fear draining his narrow face of blood. He stared at the man crouched slightly behind the thinning gunsmoke, reading correctly the deadliness in those cold blue eyes.

"Don't ever make a play like that behind my back again," Dave warned grimly. His had been a lucky shot, but no one in the crowd knew that.

Duke Mason made no comment. He reached slowly in his breast pocket for a handkerchief and as slowly brought it up to his bloody ear; a dark and ugly hate began to crowd the fear from his eyes.

There was a stir among the shocked men at the tables, and the lean man with the town marshal's badge pinned to his black shirt stepped out. Dave looked at him and reflected that the lawman had stayed clear of trouble until this moment.

The marshal paused less than ten feet from Chance, and his gaze settled coldly on the tall stranger.

"A fast gun with a mean temper," he stated coldly. "A stranger in town looking for trouble." He waited for Dave to answer him, but Chance just looked him over with cool disinterest.

"You're the kind we can do without in Paydirt!" the marshal snapped, nettled by Dave's silence. "I'll let you have one more drink; then I'll personally escort you to the end of town!"

Dave shook his head. "You sound plumb unreasonable," he protested. "I see the badge on your shirt, but I don't recollect being introduced."

The marshal's eyes narrowed. "The name's Sol Lengo," he said, "and as you say, you can plainly see the badge on my shirt. I'm the marshal of Paydirt, and I call the turn on who is welcome in town!"

"A right high-handed lawman," Dave murmured. "And a poor way to welcome a stranger."

A movement at the bar rail caught Dave's attention. From the corner of his eye he saw Packy Shane come to his hands and knees, look at Dave with burning hatred, and push himself to his feet.

The muzzle of Dave's gun stopped the fighter's lunge toward him. Packy froze, balanced on the balls of his feet, the snarl freezing on his lips.

"Once is enough for the evening," Dave observed shortly. "You've had your fun, and I've had mine. With the permission of the young marshal of Paydirt, I'll have my drink now and amble on —"

"Out of town!" Lengo put in harshly.

"Out of here," Dave corrected quietly. "I've business in Paydirt. I'll leave when I'm through with it."

Lengo eyed the gun in Dave's hand.

"You'll leave when I tell you to leave!" the marshal said, and his voice was tight and deadly. "And I'm telling you right —"

The batwings slammed against the wall, interrupting him with their abrupt clatter. He took a step back and turned, crouching slightly; then he eased up, his brow taking on a puzzled frown as Sheriff Soltight paced into the room.

The sheriff was followed by the small man in the rumpled black suit. They came into the gambling hall with the sheriff holding a cocked gun in his right fist. The small man was armed with a twin-barreled shotgun.

Soltight swung about as he spotted the marshal by the bar. He stopped, taking in the situation with one glance. His muzzle lifted, centering on Dave Chance.

His voice was a deep rumble. "You own that big roan stud anchored in front of Delaney's?"

Dave put his attention on Soltight, knowing what was bothering the lawman. He was caught in the middle here, between the sheriff and the marshal, and he had reason to distrust both.

"Yeah — that big stud's mine," he said clearly.

Sheriff Soltight scowled. "If you claim that roan, then you know why I'm asking," he said. "Irving Ramsey's across his saddle. Accountant for the Lucky Cuss mine. He's dead!"

"So he is." Dave nodded. "That's why I brought him to town."

There was a murmuring among the men and women in the gambling hall. Sol Lengo's eyes shifted to the sheriff; then his gaze flitted to the small man with the shotgun.

"Ramsey disappeared yesterday morning," the sheriff said grimly. "He was on his way to the Lucky Cuss mine with a twenty-thousand-dollar payroll. He jumped the train somewhere between here and Tumbling Brook Gorge with the money." He paused and took a deep breath. "Reckon it's your turn, stranger, to do some explaining. Where did you run into Ramsey?"

24

"Up by the creek, just south of the hills, where it makes a small pool —" He described the place. "Ramsey was on the run from somebody and tried to borrow my cayuse —"

He watched the sheriff's square, tough face as he outlined what had happened in a few terse phrases. He concluded flatly, "I didn't know who he was, Sheriff. Never saw him in my life. But he had mentioned Paydirt, and as I was headed this way, I thought I'd pack his body along." Dave made a small gesture. "I stopped by your office, and your daughter mentioned I would find you here —"

Sheriff Soltight's brows knitted. "Story sounds honest," he muttered. He turned to the small man behind him. "What do you think, Doc? A fool might pack a man he had just killed into town and try to bluff his way out of it. But this jasper doesn't strike me as that kind of a fool."

"You're wrong, Sheriff!" Duke Mason cut in harshly. "Only a fool would walk in here and do what he did."

The sheriff put his hard gaze on the gambler. "Do what?"

Packy Shane took a long step torward Dave Chance, his humiliation riding him like a sharp prod. "Put that gun away, tinhorn, and I'll break you in two! Give me five minutes, man to man —"

The sheriff lifted his glance from Duke to the raging fighter, noting the swelling on Packy's jaw, the slight cut on his lip. Then he looked at Duke again, measuring the man's hate, the handkerchief pressed to his left ear. The sheriff turned back to the marshal.

"What happened in here, Sol? Doc and I heard a shot just as we came back across the bridge."

"I didn't see all of it," Lengo answered sharply. "But it looks like this big hombre cold-cocked Packy at the bar, then drew on Duke when Duke called him on it."

"Just a minute, Marshal!" Dave protested. "For a lawman, you sure ride a rough spur on strangers. I was walking away from trouble when that tinhorn pulled a gun on me. And unless they're all liars, any man in this room can back me up on it!"

The sheriff put his questioning gaze on the marshal. "That the way it was, Sol?"

The young marshal shrugged. "I didn't see all of it," he said sullenly.

A happy grin lifted the corners of the sheriff's mouth. "Mebbe you didn't know what you were doing, fella," he said to Dave. "But you got off to a good start in this town. You always look for trouble first thing, Mac?"

Dave shook his head. "The name's Dave," he said shortly. "And there ain't a more peaceable man in town," he protested. "I'll prove it." He thrust his gun into its holster and held up his hands.

Packy started for him, a curse on his lips. The sheriff's quick-shifting Colt muzzle stopped him. "Some other time," he growled. "I'll be glad to see it."

He turned to Dave. "What this town needs is a few more peaceable hombres like you, Dave. My son Rick will be laid up for a spell, and I've got a deputy's badge on my desk. I'll be right pleased if you'd accept it, and I'll make sure the pay is right."

Sol Lengo whirled on the sheriff. "You're riding a slim limb, Bill! What do you know about this big jasper? Who is he? What's he doing in Paydirt? For all we know, he might be wanted in a dozen counties —"

"He gave Packy a taste of his own medicine," Soltight growled. "And he bucked Duke right here in his own place. That's recommendation enough for me, Sol."

Lengo's jaw ridged. "I hate to call you a darn fool, Bill!" he said grimly. "But that ain't enough for me!"

The sheriff ignored him. He turned to the small, mild-mannered man with the shotgun. "How about you, Doc?"

Doctor Robert Sonner shrugged. He was wearing gold-rimmed spectacles, and his eyes blinked as he studied Dave. "This kind of thing is out of my line," he said cautiously. "But he looks like the kind of man we could use in Rick's place," he admitted.

Chance shook his head. "Thanks for the offer, Sheriff." He stared at the tough young marshal and caught the implacable enmity in the man's cold eyes. He grinned tightly. "Might take you up on that deputy's badge later, if my business in town doesn't pan out."

The sheriff looked disappointed. "I'll have to ask you to come along with me now," he said. "I'll need you to sign a statement about what happened out at the creek."

Dave nodded. He turned to the bar, ignoring Packy, and finished his drink. He put a silver half-dollar on the bar to pay for it and swung away to join the sheriff.

Duke's thin voice reached across the quiet room as Dave and the sheriff neared the doors.

"A deputy's badge ain't going to change anything, mister! You stay out of this side of town! Cross that bridge again, and you'll be a dead man!"

Dave measured the gambler's threat and nodded grimly. "If I come across that bridge again, I'll remember that!"

CHAPTER
FOUR

Laura Soltight said, "Keep still," and held a cold compress to Rick's swollen face. She was two years older than her brother and she had an older sister's bossiness toward him. But her lips trembled a little as she saw him wince and slide down in his chair, and on impulse she ran a hand through his damp, curly hair.

"Rick, you fool, you fool —" she murmured.

They were alone in the sheriff's office. Her father and Doctor Sonner had brought Rick in, and the doctor had advised her to use a wet towel on his facial bruises until he returned. There was something going on across the river, but they had not taken the time to tell her about it. Now she waited, trying to keep her thoughts free of depressing speculation.

She heard a man's tread on the boards outside and knew he was coming in before his boots grated on the threshold. She turned to see who it was, and her hand pressed hard against Rick's face. Her brother smothered a groan and pushed her hand away.

"Cripes, sis," he mumbled, "you hurt worse than —"

He looked past Laura to the well-dressed man who had paused in the doorway. He frowned. "Hi, Johnny," he greeted him lukewarmly.

Johnn Cruze came into the law office, holding a pearl gray Stetson in his hands. He was a round-faced, clean-shaven man of thirty odd years, but he didn't look a day over twenty-five. The little gray at his temples was brushed back and lost in the waves of his brown hair. He had a boyish, ageless face that wore well.

He was in charge of operations at the Lucky Cuss mine and owner of the short-haul Devil's Canyon Railroad, and as such he was a political power in the county.

He said: "Good evening, Laura," and smiled like a man waiting to be forgiven. When she didn't answer, he came into the room to stand beside her.

"Heard you tried to whip Packy Shane," he said to Rick. He surveyed the younger man's battered face with a professional eye. "You look like you tangled with a herd of stampeding cattle."

Rick shoved himself up in the straight-backed chair. He didn't like Johnny Cruze. His swollen lips twisted in a defiant grimace. "Next time I'll —"

"There'll be no next time!" his sister cut him off firmly. She turned to Johnny, her cheeks reddening. "At least Rick was man enough to fight for what he wanted!"

"I've never doubted Rick's courage, Laura," Johnny said quickly; "only his wisdom." He saw her stiffen resentfully, and he reached out and put a hand gently on her arm. "I don't mean to be unkind. But Packy Shane is a professional fighter. Rick never was in his class. It was foolish of him even to try."

"Thanks," Rick mumbled. "Remind me to have you in my corner next time."

"I might have done you some good," Johnny said, nettled. Then he turned to Laura. "I'm sorry. I wish I could have helped. But I didn't even know."

"None of this concerns you!" she snapped.

"Anything that touches you concerns me," he replied. He was serious now. "Things haven't been the same with us for some time. You've avoided me. Is it because —?"

She turned away from him, using the towel on her brother's face to gain composure. Rick's smothered voice protested through the towel, and she eased her pressure on it.

"There's nothing I have to say to you," she told him. "You've gotten what you were after, haven't you? You don't need *us*."

"I don't need your father," he corrected her bluntly. The hard layer beneath his surface good nature showed briefly, and was immediately gone behind the boyish smile. "Laura, what are we quarreling about? If there is anything I've done —"

He turned to face the door as Sheriff Soltight's deep voice rumbled in the darkness just outside. "Give him a good going-over, Doc. If he's got a couple of busted ribs —"

His solid bulk filled the doorway of the law office. He brought up short as he saw Johnny standing by Laura; he measured the Lucky Cuss superintendent with quick hostility.

31

Dave Chance was just behind the sheriff. He moved aside and saw Johnny and went still, not believing what he saw. He had searched for this man for more than two years, never really sure that he would find him.

He saw Johnny Cruze turn pale. He stepped back, getting Laura and Rick in front of him. Then he waited, his eyes moving from Dave to the sheriff, who was eyeing him with scowling displeasure.

Doctor Sonner was the only one seemingly unaffected by Johnny's presence in the law office. He pushed past the sheriff, ignored Johnny, and set his shotgun down under the rifle rack. He walked directly to Rick, disregarding the quarrel shaping up, and started to examine the sheriff's battered son.

Bill Soltight's voice was hostile. "What in blazes are you doing in my office, Johnny?"

Johnny Cruze was looking at Dave. He made a little pacifying gesture. "I came to see Laura. And I wanted to have a talk with you about the last payroll."

"I told you to keep away from my daughter!" Soltight said grimly. He came into the office now, and behind him his shadow made a thick dark pattern on the wall. "I told you to stay away from here, unless you have official business to discuss!"

"This *is* business!" Johnny said coldly. "I'm facing a shutdown at the Lucky Cuss if I don't get a payroll through to the men up there. I want to know if you've run down any leads on Irv Ramsey?"

"Sure! I've got a lead on your embezzling accountant!" Soltight sneered. He waited, enjoying the look of puzzlement that furrowed Johnny's brow.

32

"Ramsey's dead! His body's in Corbin's back room right now, waiting to be buried. This is the hombre who brought him in."

He turned to Dave then, frowning slightly. "Never did ask you your name, fella. You do have one?"

Dave nodded. He was watching Johnny, enjoying the faint beads of sweat he could see on Johnny's face. He had found his crooked manager after two years — he could take his time dealing with him.

"Chance," he said casually in reply to the sheriff. "Dave Chance."

Johnny Cruze licked his lips. Doctor Sonner straightened briefly from his examination of Rick's bruises; he gave Dave a quick, hard scrutiny.

The sheriff waved a big hand toward Johnny. "Dave," he introduced him, "this is Johnny Cruze. Mr. Cruze's the big wheel at the Lucky Cuss mine up on Big Lars. He's the sole owner of the Devil's Canyon Railroad."

A deep-seated resentment crept into his voice. "An up and coming man, Dave. A real clever galoot. Knows what he's after and knows how to get it. We used to be partners," he added almost as an afterthought.

Johnny's glance shifted from the sheriff to Dave's cold, impassive face. He looked like a man whipsawed. He said stiffly: "I didn't want to dissolve our partnership, Bill —"

"I did!" the sheriff admitted grimly. "I know a freeze-out when I'm caught in one!" His eyes held a kindling rancor. "You got any more business here?"

Johnny mopped the sweat from his face. "Just one thing, Sheriff. I'd like to know where Dave — Mr. Chance — found Ramsey?"

Dave told him. "He was a poor horse thief," he summarized. "But he was on his way to Paydirt when I met him."

"Did he have any money with him?"

Dave eyed Johnny Cruze with a bleak smile. "He was on the run," he said coldly, "and he was traveling light. No, I didn't find any money on him. I didn't search him."

Johnny's gaze seemed to hold a desperate appeal. "I'm not doubting you, Mr. Chance." He attempted a smile, but it didn't come off well. He turned to the sheriff. "I'll drop by the funeral parlor and arrange for Ramsey's burial," he said quietly.

The sheriff shrugged. "He was your man," he growled.

Johnny's lips tightened. "He was a citizen of Paydirt, and he was murdered," he pointed out. "As such he is your responsibility, too, Sheriff!"

Bill Soltight took a threatening step toward him. "Are you implying that I —"

Johnny Cruze sidestepped him. He turned to Dave, nodding. "Thanks for bringing Ramsey's body in, Mr. Chance, and for telling me about the rope marks on his wrists. I never believed Ramsey willingly stole that payroll." He licked his dry lips as Dave made no acknowledgement. "If there is any way in which I can repay you —"

34

"I'm considering it," Dave murmured. "Where did you say you were staying in town?"

"At the Canyon House," Johnny Cruze said. "I'll be glad to see you any time, Mr. Chance."

"The name's Dave," the tall fighter said. "Some people call me 'Last Chance.'"

It got home to Johnny Cruze. But the verbal thrust was lost on the sheriff. He stepped toward Johnny and jerked a thumb in the direction of the door. "If you're through?" he suggested harshly.

Johnny stepped past him, but paused in the doorway. "I'll be in my room at the Canyon House until tomorrow morning, Sheriff," he said coldly. "You've got Dave's story and Ramsey's body. And even a blind man should see that it is no longer a simple case of embezzlement. I want to know what you're going to do about the missing payroll. And I don't have too much time to wait."

The sheriff's thick chest swelled; his neck tendons bulged. "Get to blazes out of here!" he spluttered.

CHAPTER
FIVE

The Canyon House was a big red brick structure, almost elegant in its appointments. Leaving his horse in the stables down the street, Dave stepped into the wide, carpeted lobby flanked on the window side by leather-backed settees, a half-dozen potted palms strategically placed, and a big marble-topped table in the middle of the floor space on which the *St. Louis Dispatch* and the *Houston Chronicle* of fairly recent vintage were displayed.

Dave crossed over to the hotel desk and signed for a room. The desk clerk read his name, and his voice rose with professional interest. "Oh, Mr. Chance, I have something for you."

He turned to the bank of pigeonholes at his back and from one of them took a sealed envelope which he handed over to Dave. The big man glanced at his name penned across the face of it, recognized Johnny's handwriting and thrust the envelope in his pocket. He took his key and his warbag and went across the lobby to the wide staircase.

His room was on the second floor, at the far end of the hall. His footsteps made no noise on the worn carpeting — his long shadow flickered silently along the dimly lighted walls. He opened his door and closed it, and the closeness of the room brought him to the lone window, which he tugged open. A damp breeze sifted through the lace curtains. He pulled the shade down and stepped away from it, striking a match.

He found a china-based lamp on a bedside table. Lighting the wick, he turned the glare up and gave the room a casual survey. It was like a hundred others he had slept in over the long years, better than most, yet impersonal in its appointments.

He stood in front of the dresser mirror, not seeing his image but the shadowy passage of those years. A restlessness worked up in him, leaving a flat distaste in its wake, and a desire to get out of the room. He had wasted ten years of his life and, searching the face in the mirror now, he saw only the small white scar over his eye and the slightly flattened nose and harsh mouth. He had two dollars in his pockets, an empty gut, and there wasn't a person in the world who gave a rap whether Dave Chance lived or died.

Two dollars for ten years of his life!

He reached in his pocket for Johnny's envelope. Johnny Cruze had come a long way since that day in Montana. He had been Dave's manager for years, but Dave knew now that he had never really known Johnny: an educated man with a clever tongue and an ambition to make a fast buck. He was always using his end of the purse, or his winnings, to take a gamble on something else — on stocks, on a shaky business venture. He was always going to "hit it big," and Dave would share in it.

Dave's big fist knotted. Johnny had obviously struck it rich here. And ten thousand dollars was little enough for the five hard years Dave had given him. Two thousand a year . . .

He read Johnny's note. It was short and to the point. *I'm in Room 205. I have some business to attend to. But I'll be in before midnight. I'll be waiting for you then.*

It was signed: *Johnny Cruze.*

Dave crumpled the note and burned it and the envelope in the big earthenware washbasin. He blew out the light, scattered the ashes out of the open window, and went downstairs.

The hotel dining room was closed. He stepped out to the shadowy porch and let his attention drift along the dark street that ran like a tunnel, flanked by lighted windows and occasional street lanterns hung on corner posts.

Devil's Creek made its rushing noise above the general clamor of the town, and, listening, Dave heard the heavy sighing of the Devil's Canyon engine on the siding by the depot.

Paydirt, he saw, lay along the north side of the entrance to Devil's Canyon. The rails of the Santa Fe spur which fed into Paydirt glinted in the night darkness past the depot. They ran across the emptiness of the sloping plain toward the darkness of the southeast.

The Mallet 2-4-4 engine bellowed suddenly in the night, and its drive wheels spun on the iron rails.

Couplings clanged, and the train began to move. A long spear of light stabbed into the canyon darkness.

Dave rolled a cigaret and lighted it, a tall, thick-shouldered man in the shadows. In ten years he had walked the streets of a hundred towns like this. But tonight he had the feeling there was a difference. His mind brought up the mental image of a girl standing in the doorway of the sheriff's office, staring toward the bridge across Devil's Creek. He remembered her voice, and his impression of her was clearer than that of any other woman he had been with.

He threw what was left of his cigaret into the street and walked south, toward the depot, until he saw a lighted window with "Pot of Gold Cafe" painted across it.

The Mallet engine was booming heavily now, its noise magnified as it entered the narrow confines of the canyon. It would be heard for a long time, as it labored up the twisting grade to the mines on Big Lars.

At this late hour the Café was empty. A tall broomstick individual was sweeping up among the few tables. He came around the counter as Dave took one of the stools.

"Just hash left," he said tiredly, and Dave nodded. "Coffee now," he ordered.

He was halfway through his hash when Doctor Sonner came in and sat down on the stool next to him. Close up, the medic looked old and tired. There was a seamy, unkempt air about him as he ran fingers through his thinning brown hair. His eyes seemed to hold a vague disquiet as they appraised Dave from behind his spectacles.

"Saw you come in and decided to join you in a cup of coffee," he explained.

Dave nodded. "How's young Soltight?"

Sonner shrugged. "He'll be all right. Don't know yet how much damage Shane did to his kidneys, but he's got a couple of fractured ribs. His face will heal faster, though it looks worse." He smiled pensively. "At Rick's age, a man can take a lot of punishment and still come back strong."

"Yeah," Dave agreed. He was picking at his hash, but somehow his hunger had left him. "It's not the bruises, but the scars on a man's pride that beat him, Doc." He grinned fleetingly as he reached for his coffee mug. "Rick's a big strong boy, but he doesn't belong in a ring with Shane. He doesn't throw a punch; he clubs it —"

He stopped talking as the counterman came over with a mug of coffee for Sonner. The doctor picked it up and sipped the bitter, scalding brew.

"You a professional pugilist?" he asked suddenly, his eyes lifting over his mug, appraising Dave.

Dave shrugged. "I've done some fighting," he admitted.

"You've got the look of a fighter," Sonner said. "That scar over your eye, the way the tissue ridges up —" He made a slight motion with his free hand. "No offense, Dave. But you puzzle me. A man who could knock out Shane with one punch —"

"It was a sucker punch," Dave said quietly. "I should have kept out of it."

"Shane's a bad man to have as an enemy," Sonner agreed. He smiled wanly. "I'm not a betting man, Dave. But I've got a thousand dollars saved up I'd like to bet if you'd agree to a match with Shane. It would be a sell-out."

"I quit fighting professionally a year ago," Dave said. "Sorry."

"Oh!" Doc Sonner glanced down at Dave's holstered gun. "You're quite adept with that Remington, too," he said cautiously. "New line of work?"

"It's easier on the face," Dave answered thinly. He didn't like the doctor's probing. But the small man seemed harmless and eager to be companionable.

"Thought you were in that sort of business," Sonner said. "And I'm thinking of the sheriff now. He's been getting nowhere with the trouble here. Sometimes I think he's not too interested in doing anything about it." He sipped his coffee again, and then added quickly, "Oh, Bill's doing what he can, I guess. I don't blame him if he's been working overtime combing these hills for the men who've been trying to sabotage the mines and the railroad, after the raw deal he got from Johnny Cruze."

"The man I met in the law office?" Dave asked, straight-faced. At Sonner's nod he added innocently: "Struck me as a nice enough sort."

"Johnny's a smooth article," the doctor said coldly. "I've run across his type before. He's out to make all he can here, before the mines peter out again. And he'll play both ends against the middle, too." Sonner suddenly banged his mug down on the counter with a wry gesture. "I feel like a traitor, Dave. Here I am running off at the mouth about the man I work for." He caught Dave's narrowing glance and added apologetically: "I'm the company doctor. I go up to the mines on Big Lars two or three times a week. I don't have much of a practice in town. A young doctor name of Harry Kleeman handles most of the cases in Paydirt."

Dave said curiously: "I thought you were the only doctor in Paydirt. Something Ramsey said —" He saw the doctor's eyes widen behind his glasses. "Ramsey was dying when I bent over him," Dave explained. "He asked for you."

"For me?" Doctor Sonner sighed. "I knew Irv Ramsey well, of course. Wish I could have done something for him." He got up, put a quarter on the counter and said: "Hope you decide to take that deputy's job, Dave. Bill's a stubborn sort and not too well liked here, especially by the tough element across the river. He could use a man like you as his deputy."

Dave shrugged. "If my business doesn't pan out, Doc, I may take the sheriff up on his offer."

The doctor lingered. "Mining business?"

Dave reached inside his pocket and fingered two silver dollars. "In a way," he said evenly. "I expect an old claim of mine to start paying off — ten thousand dollars' worth."

He saw sharp, puzzled surprise flash across Sonner's face. But the man was shrewd enough to know when to quit. He nodded. "Hope it works out for you, Dave."

42

Dave watched the slight, somewhat stoop-shouldered man go out. He finished his coffee, and while waiting for a refill he made himself another smoke.

Johnny Cruze was in trouble here, but this didn't concern him. All he wanted was a few minutes with his ex-manager and payment for the back wages due him.

He glanced at the clock on the wall just before it struck eleven-thirty. It was time he was getting back to the hotel.

He put his two dollars on the counter and slid off the stoool, a hard smile on his lips. A man about to come into ten thousand dollars could afford a dollar tip.

The hallway carpeting was just thick enough to deaden Dave's footsteps. A light at the end of the hallway cast a flickering illumination. From behind a door ahead of Dave a man's voice whined pettishly: "Letty, I told you I didn't have more than two drinks . . ."

Dave went on to his room, but he didn't go inside. Room 205 was near the head of the stairs, but a bend in the staircase would hide him from anyone watching below.

He had come back to the Canyon House alone, but he had the vague feeling he was being watched, and he didn't want to be seen entering Johnny Cruze's room. This business was between him and Johnny.

He came back along the hallway. A man snored loudly in one of the rooms he passed. Behind the door of 210, Letty's strident voice was audible, overriding her husband's weak protests.

Dave paused in front of 205. He put his hand on the knob and glanced down at his feet. There was a quarter-inch crack between the door and the sill, yet no light shone through. Suspicion put a cold light in Dave's eyes.

Johnny Cruze would hardly be waiting for him in the dark!

Dave turned the knob slightly and then waited. Inside the room he heard someone stir, a small shifting of a body in a chair. The silence that followed held a palpable warning to the grim-faced man.

He turned the knob with a quick movement of his wrist and shoved the door open. In the same instant he flattened his body against the wall beside the door jamb.

The muzzle blast from the shotgun split the darkness of Johnny's room. Buckshot splintered the panels of the door across the hall.

The muzzle blast lighted up the darkness enough to give Dave a glimpse of a whiskered, surly-featured man sitting in a chair facing the door, and the vague impression of a body lying across the bed.

Dave's Remington was in his hand, exploding, before the room went dark again. Inside, a man grunted, as if the wind had been smashed out of him. Then a chair overturned, and there was the sound of a body hitting the floor boards.

Dave stepped inside the dark room before the heavy reports faded. Powdersmoke made an acrid smog in the room. He turned quickly, and his fingers sought for, and found, the bolt on the inner side of the door. He closed the door and bolted it and turned fast . . . From the middle of the room came a faint and aimless stirring that faded in a man's gusty sigh of death.

Dave crossed to the bed. He struck a match and looked down to Johnny's sprawled figure. The man was breathing. The match went out, and he dropped the charred wood on the floor and stood by the bed, momentarily baffled. Then he bent over Johnny and touched the man's face and felt it was warm under his fingers. A pulse beat steadily at Johnny's temples.

A stickiness clung to Dave's exploring fingers. He traced the path of the blood up to a small gash over Johnny's left ear, and then Johnny stirred and groaned.

Dave nodded to himself. "Slugged and left to bait the trap. Someone knew I was coming up here —"

There was a loud trampling of feet in the hallway outside and a rising murmur of voices. Muted, but rising harshly above them, came the voice of the town marshal, Sol Lengo.

Dave backed away from the bed and crossed to the window in three quick strides. He looked down into a dark alley and judged that it was all of fifteen feet down. He shoved the sash up higher and slid across the sill.

He heard Lengo's voice clearly now, hard and impatient. Then someone hammered on the bolted door. Dave grinned bleakly and dropped just as a shot blasted through the door.

He landed lightly on flexed legs and was running down the alley before Lengo broke into Johnny's room. Dave came alongside the shed which flanked his room window and, jumping up, hauled himself onto the flat, tar-brushed roof.

He crouched there, hearing a confused clamor coming from Johnny's room. He knew he'd be shot if he was seen there, but he knew, too, that this ambush had been planned and that he would have had a tough time explaining to Sol Lengo if he had remained in his ex-manager's room.

He couldn't understand who would go to the trouble of setting an ambush for him, unless it was Johnny Cruze — and he didn't put this above the man who had left him stranded in Montana. But the lump behind Johnny's ear had been real, and if Johnny had staged this, he was putting a lot of emphasis on realism.

Dave was glad he had left the window open. He measured the six feet of space separating him from the window sill and jumped. His fingers closed over the wood, and his body made a small thump against the building side. He pulled himself up and into the room and then closed the window quietly.

He stood in the dark, a big, dangerous man planning his next move. Drawing his Remington, he blew through the muzzle and slipped fresh cartridges into the chamber. Then he pulled his shirt off, rumpled his hair and lighted the lamp by the bed. He pulled the covers back, pounded the pillow, sat down on the edge of the bed and took off his gunbelt. He was holding the belt and holstered gun in his hand, buckling it back on, as he opened his door and stepped out into the hallway.

He saw a small group of men clustered around Johnny Cruze's door, looking in. In the doorway of

210, a big, heavy-boned woman in a wool wrapper towered over a small, wiry man.

Sol Lengo stalked out, shoving men aside with angry impatience. He saw Dave and stopped. His weight shifted easily to the balls of his feet, and his body slid into a slight crouch.

"Where have *you* been?" he asked softly. But the gentleness in his voice was belied by the look in his yellow-green eyes.

"In my room," Chance replied. "I heard shooting and came out to see what the ruckus was about."

Lengo's voice whipped out harshly: "Like fun you were! There's a dead man in here, and someone —"

"He's right, Marshal!" the big-boned woman cut in stridently. "This man just came out of his room." She sniffed. "How people are expected to sleep with all these goings-on I don't know!" She turned to the small man at her elbow. "I'm not going to stay in town another minute, Joshua —"

Dave pushed past the town marshal and looked inside Johnny's room. Johnny Cruze was sitting on the bed, his head in his hands. The bewhiskered ambusher lay on the floor beside the overturned chair. Across the room, curtains moved to the breeze coming in through the open window.

There was a stir among the men in the hallway, and Doc Sonner came through into the room. He looked tired and disturbed and vaguely angry about something. He glanced at the man on the floor, but he didn't bother to check closer. He turned to Lengo. "What happened here, Sol?"

The marshal lifted his shoulders. He was eyeing Dave Chance with a baffled, unfriendly stare. He couldn't prove anything against this big man, and it seemed to irritate him.

"I happened to be in the lobby when I heard a shotgun go off, Doc," he said. "Ran up here and found the door locked. When I broke through, I found this jasper dead and Mr. Cruze laying across the bed. Looked like someone busted him across the skull with a gun!"

Sonner frowned. He turned to Johnny and probed the gash over the man's ear with professional interest. "You'll have a bad headache for a few hours," he said, "but not much more. I'll send someone up here with some pills. They'll help the headache."

Johnny pushed the doctor's hand away and stood up. His eyes, dark with pain, met Dave's; then he turned to the town marshal.

"I told you what happened," he said thickly. "I heard a knock on my door and opened it. I didn't see who hit me. I don't know who the man was — I don't even know if he —" he gestured to the body on the floor — "is the same man, or who killed him. I have no idea what went on in here."

Lengo wasn't satisfied with this. His yellowish gaze was like a stalking cat's, cold and unwinking, moving from Johnny to Dave Chance.

"Someone killed another man in this room," he pointed out. "Killed him and went through your window. And you say you didn't see him?"

Johnny's lips flattened. "No."

48

Lengo turned on Dave with a curt gesture toward the man on the floor. "You know this hombre?"

Dave shook his head. "I'm a stranger in Paydirt," he reminded the marshal.

Lengo sucked in an unbelieving breath. "I haven't forgotten!" he snarled. He turned to the men clustered around the door. "All right; let's get this body out of Mr. Cruze's room, down to Dade's Funeral Parlor."

He waited until the body had been carried out. Then he turned to Dave again. "For a stranger in town, you seem to have a nose for trouble."

"Cut it, Marshal!" Johnny Cruze snapped. "If you've got a quarrel with this man, take it outside. If you'll excuse me, gentlemen, I want to be alone!"

Lengo whirled on him, an angry retort thinning his lips. But Doctor Sonner checked him. "Let's go, Marshal," he said briskly. "Mr. Cruze is right. He needs quiet."

Dave followed them out to the hall. Behind them, Johnny closed the door firmly. Dave's jaw tightened slightly. He tapped Lengo on the shoulder.

"You have anything more to say to me?"

Lengo gritted his teeth. "Yeah. I don't like your face, feller — or your habits! I don't like anything about you! And hombres I don't like I'm suspicious of. You may be innocent, but I doubt it. Someone killed that whiskered gent in Johnny Cruze's room, and I don't have to strain my brain to know it was you —"

"Why?" Dave cut in coldly. "Why are you so sure I would kill a man I don't even know?"

"I ain't so sure you didn't know him!" Lengo snapped. "And I don't give a hoot in Hades *why* you killed him. But I'm telling you this much right now! I'm giving you a week to take care of your business here. Then I want you out of town! Get that, big boy! A week!"

He turned on his heel. Doctor Sonner looked after the marshal until Lengo had passed out of sight down the staircase. The he turned to Dave. He made a small gesture of helplessness.

"Sol's a lot like the sheriff," he ventured. "Plumb set in his ways — and a good deal more dangerous. I wouldn't cross him."

Dave shrugged. "I never cross a man unless he stands in my way. You might tell the marshal that. He'll draw his pay longer."

An odd gleam came into Doctor Sonner's pale eyes, and he nodded stiffly.

"I'll try to reason with him," he said softly. Then he turned and followed the marshal down the stairs.

CHAPTER
SIX

Johnny Cruze was sitting in an overstuffed chair when Dave Chance came in. The big man closed the door softly behind him. It was past midnight, and the hotel had settled down for the night. But across the river the sounds of merriment continued, punctuated by an occasional gunshot fired at the stars by some tipsy celebrant.

Johnny looked at Dave through sick eyes. "Expected you," he muttered. "That's why I left the door unlocked."

"Thanks," Dave said dryly. He crossed to Johnny, reached down and grabbed a fistful of shirt and coat. He jerked the smaller man up and held him, squirming, close to his hard, smoldering eyes.

"I've waited two years for this," he grated. "You were always good with words. Start talking! Tell me about that day in Butte."

Johnny's face darkened as blood congested in it. He tried to twist free. His voice was thin and protesting. "Let — me — down — Dave —"

Dave shoved him back into the chair. He stood over the man, big fists knotted. "Owner of a railroad, eh? Big shot in town! Manager of a million-dollar silver mine!"

Dave's lips curled unbelievingly. "Where did you learn about mining, Johnny? From my corner, when we fought in mining camps?"

"I — I studied engineering — in college," Johnny gasped. He was getting his breath back, but his headache was pounding so heavily he squinted from the pain of it.

"Didn't know you ever studied anything," Dave sneered, "except how to double-cross your friends!"

Johnny lifted a protesting hand. "Dave — I meant to get in touch with you." He was getting his composure back, and his words came easier. "I finally ran into a streak of luck out here, Dave. I hit it big. But I was thinking of you — believe me! I tried to locate you —"

Dave reached down and jerked Johnny erect again. "You're a liar!" he growled.

Johnny raised his right hand, palm outward, as though taking an oath. "Dave — I swear it! I owe this break to you. It was *our* money — yours and mine — that made this possible." He paused to get his breath and move back as Dave's fingers relaxed.

"When I left Butte with our winnings, I wanted to use that money as a stake — for both of us. I didn't really mean to run out on you, Dave. But you know how it was that afternoon. Half of Butte's citizens lost a good part of their shirts betting on Butte's pride and joy. When you licked him, they were in an ugly mood. That's why I picked up our purse and gambler's stakes and left town. I had over twenty thousand dollars —"

52

"*Twenty thousand!*" Dave's jaw knotted. "You had twenty thousand — and you left me stranded, without a dollar?"

"They were in an ugly mood," Johnny whined. "Don't you remember? I was afraid we'd never get out of town with the money. Dave —" he tried to temporize — "don't you see? They were really sore at me — not you! If I could clear out of town before they got organized —"

"You left me to them!" Dave snarled. He jammed the man back into his chair. "But you're right about one thing. It was your hide they were after. Sure, they treated me rough. But the sheriff cooled them off before they got out of hand. Probably the only man in town on my side. He gave me a stage ticket out of town and a couple of dollars out of his own pocket."

Dave leaned over Johnny, his eyes glinting wickedly. "I could hardly stand after that fight. And all I got out of it was a ticket out of town — and meal money!"

Johnny took out a handkerchief and wiped the sweat from his face. "Half of what I've got here is yours, Dave! That's what I've been trying to tell you! Half of it's yours!"

"Half of what?" Dave snarled.

"Half of the Devil's Canyon Railroad!"

Dave shook his head. "I don't want half of your railroad. I don't want your troubles. Oh, I heard about them in the sheriff's office." He chuckled grimly. "This time you talk your way out of them, Johnny. All I want is ten thousand dollars from you; my half of the Butte fight money."

Johnny licked his lips. "Dave — half of what I've got here is worth more than five times that much!"

"Ten thousand dollars!" Dave repeated grimly. "I'll settle for that."

Johnny glanced at the door and licked his lips again. "I don't have it, Dave."

Dave's eyes narrowed. "I've been looking for you for two years. I want what belongs to me, Johnny. And I'll get it if I have to take it out of your hide!"

"I haven't got ten thousand dollars!" Johnny said desperately. "Not where I can lay my hands on it in a hurry." He shrank from the look on Dave's face. "It's all tied up in the railroad. Even my pay from the mine is being held up, until this payroll business is cleared."

He saw the edge of belief appear in Dave's eyes, and his words tumbled out. "The railroad could be worth a half-million, Dave, if I can hang onto it. Help me straighten things out here and I'll give you twenty thousand —"

"I thought you said half," Dave rasped.

"Half," Johnny agreed quickly.

Dave eyed the frightened man. He was thinking over what he had heard in the sheriff's office. It was possible that Johnny Cruze was telling the truth.

He turned and picked up a straight-backed chair and walked to the door with it. The marshal's bullets had ripped the bolt loose — the scars in the panels reminded him of the hard-eyed lawman who seemed so eager to make trouble for him. He propped the edge of

54

the chair under the knob and stood thinking for a moment.

Then he turned and walked back to Johnny Cruze.

"Who was the man I killed in here?"

Johnny shrugged. "Probably one of the toughs who hang out across the river." He touched the lump under his ear. "He was waiting for you, wasn't he?"

Dave nodded. "I got your note at the desk, after I left the sheriff's office. You didn't rig that ambush yourself, did you?"

Johnny shook his head. "No, Dave, I need you!" His voice sounded earnest. "I haven't got a friend in Paydirt."

Dave grinned. "What a shame! You still don't have one!"

Johnny got to his feet and steadied himself against the chair back. "I deserve that, I guess." He walked to the dresser and took two glasses and an unopened bottle of whiskey from a drawer. He uncorked the bottle and poured.

"The sheriff's trying to break me!" he said bitterly. "The marshal's a crook and a killer! I don't have a friend in town. I can't even trust my own men!"

"I'm sorry for you," Dave said. "I hurt just thinking about it."

Johnny ignored the gibe. "For the first time in my life I stand to make a pile of money. Help me out, Dave. Like old times?"

The gall of the man stopped Dave. He took the drink, considering the situation.

His grin was a little lopsided. "All right, Johnny. It's a deal." He put his glass down on the dresser and walked over to the small walnut desk in the corner. He picked up a quill pen and held it out to Johnny, who looked puzzled.

"Write it down, Johnny," he said pleasantly. "A half-interest in the Devil's Canyon Railroad."

Johnny's pride was hurt. "You don't trust me?"

"Write it all down, legal-like. And sign it!"

Johnny sighed. "You've changed, Dave. You didn't need a written contract in the old days. My word was —"

"Write it down!"

Johnny walked to the desk, found paper and penned the contract. He looked up before he signed it. "It won't be worth a dime if we go broke, Dave!"

"We won't," Dave promised. He was thinking of the long, fruitless years as he watched Johnny sign with a flourish. He read the paper, nodded, and folded it neatly before tucking it away in his coat pocket.

He walked to the dresser and emptied his whiskey glass. "All right, Johnny. We're partners. Now start at the beginning . . ."

Johnny Cruze took his whiskey glass to the chair with him. His head still ached, but he seemed more cheerful.

"Like I told you, Dave, I studied engineering. Got kicked out of school before I finished, but —" he shrugged — "that's neither here nor there, is it? Came West to make a fast buck, but my luck was all bad. I was broke the night I saw you lick that big stevedore in Natchez — remember?"

Dave nodded. "I know the rest of it," he said coldly, "up to Butte, Montana."

"Well, I had twenty thousand dollars when I left that town," Johnny continued. "I headed South — way South. Wound up in New Orleans; did some gambling for high stakes." He grinned wryly. "I thought I knew all the angles when it came to poker. But I ran across some real experts in that town . . ."

He sipped his drink. "I managed to hold onto fifteen thousand, got involved in a brawl —" He pulled up his right sleeve to show Dave a wicked ten-inch scar on his forearm. "Knife," he said laconically. "Anyway, I had to leave town in a hurry. So I headed this way and found myself in Paydirt. It was the best break of my life."

He looked at Dave. "You know anything of local history?"

Dave shook his head.

"Used to be one of the big silver-producing areas in the country," Johnny said. "About thirty million dollars' worth of ore was shipped out of here in six years time. Then, about two years ago, the mines on Big Lars started petering out. The Lucky Cuss, the biggest producer, was about to shut down."

He took a sip of his whiskey and added: "Most of the mines are on a bare ridge shelfing off Big Lars peak. No room for a town, so Paydirt came into being down here, at the head of Devil's Canyon. It's about six miles to the Lucky Cuss, as the eagle flies — but twenty-six of the toughest miles by rail or muleback."

Dave finished his whiskey and poured himself a refill.

"I poked around the Lucky Cuss, with the consent of the owners, friends of mine I had looked up in New Orleans. They were the people who got me out of town and headed me for Paydirt. I remembered some of my mining engineering, played a hunch, and cut a drift in one of the old tunnels. We hit a new vein, and it paid off."

He got up and refilled his glass. "For my lucky guess I was given some shares in the Lucky Cuss and made superintendent. It pays well. But I still had most of that fifteen thousand dollars burning a hole in my sock, and I wanted more than a few shares in a silver mine. And just about that time the people who owned the Devil's Canyon Railroad went broke."

He shrugged, looking deep into his glass. "It struck me as a good business venture at the time, Dave. I knew the Lucky Cuss would go on producing for a long time — and whoever owned the railroad would stand to make money." He smiled thinly. "Whoever owned the railroad could put the squeeze on the mines any time he wanted."

Dave eyed him. "Even on your old friends from New Orleans?"

Johnny made a deprecating gesture. "It was my hunch that kept the mine paying off. They weren't worrying about me, Dave. They were too busy with their social affairs in New Orleans."

"How did Sheriff Soltight get a partnership in the railroad?" Dave cut in coldly.

"I offered it to him," Johnny said bitterly. "He didn't have much money, but I wanted the sheriff on my side, just in case there was trouble later on. A man works harder," he added cynically, "when he's got a stake in something."

"I'll remember that," Dave said.

Johnny flushed. "The sheriff had his own little deal here before I came to Paydirt. He used to run a mule team up to the mines on Big Lars, before Fillmore and Severson built the railroad. That wiped him out. I knew how he felt about the railroad. And when I had a chance to buy them out, cheap, I told the sheriff about it. He seemed glad of the chance to come in with me."

"He swears you froze him out!" Dave recalled.

Anger drew tight lines around Johnny's mouth. "That's what's bothering me, Dave. From the first we've had trouble. Trestles burned — rail-bed blocks — engine trouble. Sheriff Soltight didn't do anything. He'd ride around and come back, and the sabotage would continue. We had words over it. Most of the time I'm busy at the mine. I depended on him to sort of keep things running on the railroad." Johnny shook his head. "Stubborn fool! First argument we had, he blew up and pulled out!"

He put his gaze on Dave, frowning slightly. "That's what made me suspicious, Dave. I didn't break up the partnership — he did. And then the last two Lucky Cuss payrolls didn't get up to the men at the mines. Both pay clerks who left Paydirt for Big Lars, on he railroad, disappeared somewhere between town and the mines."

"And you think it's the sheriff who's trying to break you?"

"I can't figure it any other way," Johnny replied grimly. "He's the only man who stands to gain if the railroad goes broke. There's always his mule train to fall back on."

Dave put his empty glass down on the dresser. "What about that bunch in the Golden Nugget?" he asked abruptly. "Duke Mason? Where does he fit in?"

Johnny spread his hands. "Right where Duke always fits — where it pays off for Duke. That's why I don't believe Duke has anything to do with my troubles. He's got a good thing in that gambling hall across the river, as long as the mines on Big Lars are paying off. Break the railroad, and the Lucky Cuss and the other outfits on Big Lars face a shutdown. And what would Duke get out of that?"

He got up and started to refill Dave's glass, but Dave put his hand over it. "I've had enough, Johnny." He moved to the door, turned. "That dead man I brought in tonight — Ramsey — you trusted him?"

"As well as I'd trust any man," Johnny muttered. "Ramsey didn't run off with that payroll, and I don't think Ed Minik, the other payroll man, did either. They both took the night train out of Paydirt, and somewhere between here and the mining camp they disappeared. I know what it looks like. It's what the sheriff believes, and most of the people here, too, for that matter: that two men succumbed to the temptation of easy money. But I think Ed and Ramsey were held up and taken off that train, although how that was done with no one noticing it —"

Dave interrupted him. "It could be they both jumped train with the money and someone else trailed them and took it from them. How much money was there in the payrolls?"

"About thirty thousand dollars."

"A lot of seemingly honest men have gone wrong over less," Dave said. "Anyone notice Ramsey on the train?"

"Several boys from the day shift were in the coach with him," Johnny answered. "They were pretty tuckered out from the day in town and didn't pay much attention to Ramsey. Doc Sonner was on the train, too. He said he and Ramsey stepped out to the rear platform for a smoke; then the doctor came inside to get away from the engine smoke."

He made an impatient gesture. "Doctor Sonner said he didn't think of Ramsey again until they reached camp. Then he was gone."

Dave frowned. "Happen the same way with the other payroll man?"

Johnny nodded. "I trusted both men. We didn't advertise the payroll, of course. The sheriff knew about it, and his son, Rick. Not too many people did. But I suppose word could have gotten around." He shook his head. "I still don't believe Ramsey tried to steal that payroll. He didn't have the nerve, for one thing. But someone is trying to break the railroad. And a breakdown on the Canyon line will cause a shutdown at the mines. I've had three wires from New Orleans already. We can't stand to lose another payroll!"

"When is your next one?"

"I'm waiting for a wire from New Orleans now, from Lee Hansen. If I don't get the money by the weekend, I face a strike at the Lucky Cuss. Some of the men have already walked off the job. And if the mines shut down, I — we go broke, Dave!"

Dave Chance knuckled his jaw in a thoughtful gesture. "Who's taking the next payroll up to the mines?"

"I am!" Johnny snapped.

Dave grinned meagerly. "I've got a better idea, partner. I'll tell you about it later.

He walked to the door and pulled away the chair. "Pleasant dreams," he murmured, and went out.

CHAPTER
SEVEN

Sheriff Soltight hiked his booted feet up on his scarred desk top and stared morosely at the town marshal, who paced angrily within the thin splash of morning sunlight coming in through the office windows. The sheriff had a hangover, and it did not improve his surly mood.

He said: "You can't prove anything on him, can you, Sol?" and felt a malicious pleasure at the bitter hardness it evoked in the marshal's eyes.

"I don't have to!" Sol snapped. "Bill, what's happened to you? You gonna let every two-bit gunman come into Paydirt and do just about what he wants?"

"He hasn't done anything I'd want him for," Bill growled. "Just what has Dave Chance done? I questioned witnesses this morning. Packy Shane tried to shove him around and got hit so fast and hard no one saw it." Pleasure rang in the sheriff's tone. "Duke tried to take a hand while Dave's back was turned and —" He raised a hand, blocking off Sol's retort. "Just a minute, Sol. Maybe you didn't see it, but a half-dozen people I talked to did. This Dave's a —"

"A fair hand with a gun!" the marshal conceded coldly. "And he took a swipe at Packy, after Packy beat the tar out of yore boy! All right; I can sympathize with you. But think a minute! We've got troubles here. Are you blind? What's a big, trouble-making jasper like Dave Chance doing in Paydirt?"

"Maybe we can ask him!" the sheriff snapped, nettled by the other's sharp words. "Just as soon as —"

"You can ask me right now!" Dave said pleasantly.

Sol Lengo whirled, his right hand dropping instinctively to the butt of his Colt. The sheriff took his feet off his desk and surveyed the big man in the doorway.

"Come on in," he invited.

Dave stepped inside the law office. He said: "If that deputy's job is still open, I'll take it, Sheriff."

Soltight came to his feet. He shot a look at the town marshal, and his lips tightened stubbornly. "You're danged right it's still open." He took a badge from his desk drawer and held it out to Dave, who pinned it to his coat.

"Raise your right hand," the sheriff instructed, and swore Dave in.

Sol's sneer was ugly as he watched. "Reckon you played yore hand close this time, feller. That star figures to give you legal status in Paydirt. But don't forget I run this town; not the sheriff's office! And what I told you still goes! Star or no star, you get out of Paydirt before the end of the week, or I'll kill you!"

"Sol!" the sheriff yelled angrily. "Are you crazy? You're riding this too hard! What have you got against Dave?"

"I don't like his looks!" Sol sneered. "Just figure it that way. And don't you crowd me, Bill!"

64

He turned and stepped away and nearly collided with Doctor Sonner coming in. "Get out of my way, Doc!" he snarled unpleasantly, and turned out of sight down the walk.

Doctor Sonner turned to look after him. Then he put his spectacled gaze on Dave Chance, moved on to the scowling sheriff.

"What's biting *him?*"

"Pride, maybe," Soltight answered. "He's got a tough job here," he said, trying to make excuses for the man. "And he doesn't take to pushing."

Dave's eyes held a far-away glint. "I'll keep out of his way," he said, "unless he corners me." Coldly: "I don't take much to pushing, either."

"A devil of a situation," Doctor Sonner observed, sinking wearily onto a chair. "Your temper isn't what could be called even, by any means," he said to the sheriff. He sighed. "If the law in Paydirt starts fighting itself —"

Dave shrugged. "I won't bother Lengo," he promised. He reached inside his pocket and brought out the mouth organ he had picked up on the rocky slope above the creek where Ramsey had died.

"Ever see this before?" he asked the sheriff.

The sheriff took it into his hands and looked it over. He shook his head, then passed it back. "Can't place it. Why?"

Dave told him. "I had a hunch the man who dropped it might be from Paydirt. If he is, and I pick him up, we might get a line on those payroll robberies."

He was watching the sheriff's face for some giveaway, but Bill's stubborn features held only a scowling displeasure. "Rick might know," he said. "The kid stuck his nose across the river a lot —" He turned to Doctor Sonner. "Ever see this before, Bob?"

The doctor shook his head. "Can't say I have. Nor," he added slowly, anticipating Dave's next question, "have I had anyone come into my office recently for treatment of a gunshot wound. Had one stabbing and two head injuries last night, but no one with a bullet in him. Or through him," he added.

"What about that other doctor you mentioned?"

"Kleeman?" Sonner's eyes blinked behind his lenses. "Harry Kleeman has his office over the Miner's Bank." Stiffly, "I don't keep track of his patients."

"Reckon I will," Dave said, turning.

"Hold on," the sheriff said. "I'll get my hat and go along with you." He turned quickly for the gray Stetson hanging on the wall hook behind him. The sudden motion made his head spin. He staggered slightly and put a hand down on the desk top and said thickly: "Reckon I'll have to pass this one up, Dave. I need a half-pot of black coffee first."

Dave was sympathetic. "It might not lead to anything, anyway. But I might as well start earning my keep."

Sonner turned to the sheriff after Dave left. "A sharp man," he observed. "And a big man —" he added thoughtfully.

Sheriff Soltight took a deep breath. He was worried now, with Sol's angry words echoing in his ears. He had

66

put a badge on a man he knew nothing about, thereby giving legal sanction to anything the big man might do.

"Let's hope he's not too big for the job, Doc," he muttered. But his tone lacked confidence.

Rick Soltight's gaze drifted to the sun shining through the kitchen window as he played the jack of clubs.

His sister said sharply: "You're not thinking at all," as she took his hand, and added succinctly: "We're playing hearts, but you don't have to look so displeased because you have to play with your sister."

"Aw, it ain't that, sis" Rick protested. His face was still puffed, and there were blue and lemon yellow blotches on his jaw and under his eyes. "Doc wound so many layers of tape around me I feel like a mummy. I ain't hurt that bad," he muttered rebelliously.

"You're hurt badly enough to stay in for a while," Laura said. She knew what was making Rick restless, and while she didn't approve, she understood. "Get well first before you try to see that girl again."

"Look who's handing out advice," Rick mumbled. "You know how Dad feels about Johnny Cruze."

Laura slammed her cards down on the table. "You mind your own business," she said inconsistently.

Rick grinned, though it hurt his face. "Maybe you'd rather have Sol Lengo come calling on you?" He saw the flash of her eyes and added bitingly: "Now there's a man Father wouldn't mind having for a son-in-law."

"And you?" she challenged.

"Me?" He shrugged. "I'm just the kid brother, sis."

"Don't evade the subject," she said grimly.

"I don't trust Sol," Rick said simply. He scowled at the card his sister had played and took it with the queen of hearts.

Rick's answer surprised Laura. For the past five years she had been the only woman in the Soltight household, and she had been both mother and big sister to her brother. It had never occurred to her that Rick even considered her emotional problems.

"What about Johnny?"

Rick kept his eyes on his cards. "What about him?" he mumbled.

"You know what I mean?"

He looked at her, his eyes suddenly level and serious. "I don't like him either," he said bluntly.

"Why? Because he and Dad broke up their partnership?"

"Because he's too smooth, sis. He can talk his way around a starving cougar in a cage —"

"Is that bad? Does a man have to be rude and uneducated for you to like him?"

Rick's eyes dropped to his cards again; his smile was boyish. "Aw, heck, sis — I don't want to get into an argument with you. If you like Johnny, it's all right with me —"

He turned at a knock on the door. "We've got a caller, sis. Might be Johnny didn't take Dad's advice to stay away."

Laura got up, reddening, and went to the door. She was thinking of Johnny Cruze, but the big man who smiled at her was not the rairoad man.

She said, unconsciously hostile: "Dad's not at home."

"I know," Dave replied. "I've come to see your brother."

She turned and looked back at Rick, a doubtful frown in her eyes. "He's really not well enough to —"

"I'm well enough for anything," Rick interrupted. "Come on in, Mister —"

"Chance," the big man said. "Dave Chance." He walked into the kitchen and looked down at Rick. "You look like you've been in a stampede," he said cheerfully. "Didn't you ever learn to duck?"

"I did," Rick said, unabashed. "Ducked into every punch he threw." He looked up at his sister, who was scowling at him. "And I'll knock Packy's head off next time." He chuckled softly as Laura turned away.

"Coffee, Mr. Chance?" she asked somewhat coldly.

Dave smiled. "Thank you, Miss Soltight."

"Aw, call her Laura," Rick said. He watched Dave settle in a chair across from him. "I heard what you did to Packy. Two punches and — wowie!" His eyes gleamed. "Give me a week working out with you, Dave, and I'll —"

"You'll leave Shane alone," Dave advised. "He's a rough customer."

"You handled him pretty easy," Rick said peevishly. "He can't be that good!"

"I hit him when he wasn't expecting it," Dave said shortly. "Don't get any false ideas about Shane from what happened last night."

Laura came to the table with a cup of steaming black coffee. "You talk like a sensible man, Mr. Chance." There was more warmth in her voice now. She indicated the badge on his vest. "I see Dad talked you into accepting the job."

Dave nodded. "I'm just filling in in Rick's place. I don't expect to hold the job down too long — just until your brother gets back on his feet."

"I'm on my feet now," Rick protested. "I don't intend to sit around playing hearts with sis all week, no matter what my father says."

Dave grinned. "Stay put for a while, anyway. Give me a chance to earn a week's pay."

Laura explained: "Rick's determined to go back across the river to see that girl he got into trouble over." She tossed her head. "Sometimes I think he's as muley as dad."

"Look who's talking!" Rick snapped. "You've been seeing Johnny, knowing how Dad feels about him —"

"Let's talk about this," Dave interrupted the family quarrel. He placed the mouth organ on the table. "Ever see this — or know of someone who plays one?"

Rick focused his attention on the harmonica. "Looks like the one Zack Miller uses. Why?"

"Who's Zack?"

"A tough character who hangs out in Barraby's Pool Hall, across the road from Duke's Golden Nugget." Rick frowned. "He's a gunslinger who drifted into Paydirt from up north two or three months ago. Generally hangs around with his partner, a reedy-looking gent

70

with a cast in his left eye and a touchy disposition. Goes by the name of Voss Garrett."

Dave burned his lips on the coffee. "Should have told you," he said to Laura. "I like my coffee cool. If you've got a chunk of ice handy —"

Rick guffawed. Laura looked offended. "Ice? In hot coffee? I've never heard of such a thing."

Dave got to his feet, pocketing the harmonica. "Most people haven't," he said gravely. "Didn't mean no offense, Miss —"

"Laura," Rick put in quickly. He was grinning, even though it hurt him. "Sis won't mind, seeing you're practically one of the family now, wearing that badge."

Laura's face reddened. "I'll try to remember you like your coffee with ice in it the next time, Mister —"

"Dave," Rick supplied impishly.

"You shut up!" his sister exploded, whirling on him.

Rick put a hand to the side of his face. "Ouch!" The pain was not altogether feigned.

Dave felt slightly uncomfortable. "Thanks for the tip," he said to Rick. "I'll pay Zack a visit."

Rick came forward in his chair and made a grimace. "Barraby's place is a tough hangout, Dave. If Zack's in there, you'll probably find Voss around. And watch Monk Barraby. He's a big, hairy jasper with sleepy eyes. Spends most of his time smoking a cigar and looking at the pictures in the *Police Gazette*. But he sees everything that goes on in his place, and he's mighty fast with a sawed-off shotgun he keeps handy under the counter."

Dave nodded. "I'll keep my eye on him."

Laura walked to the door with him. "You're as big in bright daylight as you appeared last night," she said. "Usually a man comes back to size in the morning."

He put his steady gaze on her, caught by something in her voice he couldn't quite make out. She was tall enough so that she didn't appear ridiculously small. She had an easy way of talking to a man, which was probably the result of living close to two of them. But there was a restlessness in her, a dissatisfaction he could sense.

"Those tiny bumps over your eyes," she said suddenly, "I didn't notice them last night."

"Maybe I look better in the dark," he said coldly. "Anything else about me that bothers you?"

She smiled. "Touchy, aren't you? They don't bother me, Dave. But I'm curious as to how they got there."

"Maybe I'll tell you — sometime," he said levelly. He touched his fingers to his hat. "Goodbye, Laura."

She stood in the doorway and watched him stride up the street, a big man with a light walk. She felt oddly elated, and being an honest girl, she examined the feeling.

"Laura — you're a fool!" she muttered.

Behind her Rick called, "Quit mooning over Dave, sis, and let's finish this game." He chuckled as she turned and went on with a brother's callousness: "Ain't one man enough for you, sis?"

CHAPTER
EIGHT

Dave Chance came to Canyon Road, stopped at the stable where he had left his horse and fed the animal four lumps of sugar he had swiped during breakfast in the hotel dining room.

He had charged the breakfast to Johnny Cruze and given similar instructions to the desk clerk, and Johnny had verified both. Now he thought of what the sheriff would say when he found out about it, and decided he'd take care of explaining when the time came.

He left the stables and crossed the bridge with the sun hard against his left side, glittering from the badge on his coat. He saw Sol Lengo appear in the doorway of the barbershop across the street. The marshal eyed him the way a big jungle cat eyes a rival.

Dave walked past the marshal. If the man was going to make trouble, he might as well meet it now. But Lengo, apparently, was going to wait out the week.

Barraby's Pool Hall loomed up ahead, a false-fronted, unpainted board structure that had a decided sag to the south. The windows fronting the street were dirty, and dead flies sprinkled the sills.

Dave paused in front of the door and let his gaze rest on the Golden Nugget across the street, remembering

Duke Mason's threat of last night. But an air of somnolence clung to the big gambling hall — the tired and deserted atmosphere that went with the early morning hour.

The Nugget was the kind of place that stayed open until the last paying customer went home; then the drunks were thrown out and the bar closed. Now the only sign of life around the big batwings was a mangy-looking mongrel sniffing at the heels of an uneasy swamper who had come outside to empty a bucket of dirty water.

Inside the poolroom, Dave could hear the clack of ivory balls colliding. He opened the door and stepped inside a close, smoky room that probably had not been ventilated for weeks.

The man behind the counter on the left was big and hairy, as Rick had described him. He seemed half asleep. He was sitting on a high chair over the counter, his elbows propped on it, his big hairy hands holding his head while he stared down at a spread-out magazine. A cloud of smoke drifted up from between his hands.

Dave's attention drifted from this man, who did not even glance up to see who had entered, to linger briefly on the two men playing eight ball on the near table. A big gray tomcat lay curled in the middle of the other table.

A reedy individual, gun-hung and long-faced, sat in a chair propped against the far wall. He was sliding a cue stick up and down between his hands as he waited.

74

Warning rang a bell in Dave's head as he surveyed the scene. Rick had not underrated Barraby's. A tight expectancy crinkled his eyes, and an old familiar prickling touched his shoulder muscles.

He had come here looking for Zack Miller because, obviously, Sol Lengo wouldn't have. The marshal didn't give a hoot about the Canyon line.

Dave walked over to the counter and said clearly: "Seen Zack Miller lately?"

Monk Barraby took his time lifting his face from between his hands. He rolled his cigar between his thick lips and blew smoke at Dave.

"Purty, ain't she?" he replied, grinning salaciously. He obviously meant the buxom, heavy-hipped girl in tights taking up one full page of the *Gazette*.

Dave kept his eyes on the poolroom owner's face. From the corners of his eyes he caught the exchange of glances between the two pool players. The reedy jasper, who probably was Voss Garrett, Zack's sidekick, slowly let his cue stick slide down between his feet.

"Zack Miller?" Dave repeated with level patience.

Barraby's small black eyes traveled down Dave Chance's frame from boots to hat crown. He looked pointedly at Dave's badge. "You the law?"

"I am," Dave replied calmly.

"What do you want of Zack?"

Dave reached inside his pocket and placed the harmonica on the counter. "I want to give Zack back his mouth organ."

Monk frowned. "Didn't know Zack played one of them things," he mumbled. "Knew he was a

75

windbag —" He grinned at his own joke, but Dave's face remained grave.

Monk grunted. "Reckon you'll find Zack in the back room." He jerked a thumb toward a closed door. "He's sleeping late. Zack didn't feel any too well this morning."

Dave nodded. He had a pretty good idea why Zack wasn't feeling too well. But as he turned and started for the rear door, he remained alert. He didn't like the hands-off atmosphere here — and he was was suspicious of Barraby's easy acceptance of his request.

Behind the apparent casualness of these watching men was a leashed violence, waiting for some signal to loose it.

Dave reached the back door, turned the knob, and stepped in as the door opened. It slammed against the inner wall as he stepped lightly to one side of the door frame, thereby out of reach of the guns in the pool hall. His own gun was cradled easily in his palm as he surveyed the cubbyhole lighted by a single cobwebbed window.

There was the sharp odor of carbolic salve in the enclosed space, and a fainter, sweeter smell he couldn't place. There was this mingling of unusual odors in the room — and a man lying still on the makeshift bunk under the window.

The man was fully clothed. He was on his back, and his beard-stubbled mouth hung open. It was a slack, weathered face that looked up at the ceiling, but the open blue eyes had a vacant stare. Dave Chance knew the man was dead before he bent over him.

Zack's left shoulder was bandaged, and the job had been done by a professional. But Dave guessed that it was not the shoulder wound that had killed this man.

Dave bent over the body, studying it. He could see no other marks of violence on the man other than the bandaged shoulder. But the sweetish odor was stronger as he bent over Zack. He gagged slightly and drew back, frowning.

Zack had not been dead long. His body had the limpness of recent death. And he had not died hard.

Dave turned slowly, knowing there was nothing more he could learn here. The stillness inside the poolroom warned him, brought a bleak glitter to his eyes. He stepped through the doorway, and Barraby's ominous voice halted him.

"Did you give Zack his mouth organ, Deputy?"

Dave's weight shifted imperceptibly to his toes. He felt trouble here, like a submerged reef in a sunlit lagoon. Somewhere between here and the front door they would make the play they were waiting for . . .

"Zack's dead," he said diffidently. "Reckon he won't need it now."

Voss Garrett stood up and let the cue stick fall. It made a slight thump on the floor, and it awakened the cat.

"Dead?" His voice rasped like an unresined bow across cheap violin catgut. "Zack was alive and kicking just a few minutes ago?"

"Then he cooled mighty fast," Dave answered. "He's dead. And from the looks of him, he scared himself to death."

A sneer crawled across the narrow, pinched face of Voss Garrett. "I say Zack was alive when you went into that room, mister. If he's dead, you just killed him!"

Dave's eyes were somber. "Sure," he said quietly. "I choked Zack to death with his harmonica." He balanced forward on his toes, knowing now that this trap had been set for him and there was no peaceful way out. "What do you intend to do about it?" he challenged coldly.

"Zack was my friend!" Voss snarled. "And no badge-toter can walk in and kill him —"

He drew and fired as Dave moved. But he was dying as he fired. Dave's first slug lifted him up on his toes. He twisted around at the impact, fell against the wall and slid down.

Dave whirled to face Monk. One of the two pool players threw a billiard ball in a swift underarm motion — it glanced off Dave's head. The big man staggered and fell against the corner table. Monk's shotgun blast missed him by inches. A few pellets from the outer edge of the pattern peppered his back.

Dave dropped to the floor, rolled, and another ball bounced off the boards next to his head. He came up against the wall and caught Monk leaning far over the counter, trying to follow him with the shotgun.

The shotgun blast ripped into the ceiling as Dave's bullet smashed into the hairy man. Monk slid down behind the counter, pulling the shotgun with him.

A cue stick, thrown like a spear, thudded into the wall by Dave's head. Dave thumbed his last shot at the man who threw it. The man yelled. But he went out the door at a run.

The remaining combatant changed his mind about continuing the fight. He made a break after his companion. Dave slammed the cue stick after him. It missed him by a hair and went through the window.

Braced against the wall, Dave surveyed the empty poolroom. Through the broken window he caught a glimpse of Sol Lengo, running across the street toward Barraby's.

Dave pushed himself away from the wall and made the door a moment before the marshal entered. Lengo skidded to a stop and tried to bring his drawn Colt around just as Dave's empty Remington jammed hard into his stomach.

Lengo gasped. The wind went out of him in one whoosh! His eyes rolled, and he turned green around the mouth.

Dave reached out and yanked Sol's gun out of his hand. The man seemed paralyzed, fighting to suck in air.

Dave spun the marshal around and jammed him up against the poolroom wall. The marshal sagged, his legs rubbery.

"I don't want trouble with you Marshal!" Dave snarled. "I promised the sheriff I'd steer clear of you."

Lengo's voice came in jerks. "I'll — get you — for this —"

"Save your breath," Dave advised grimly. "One of the two men who killed Irving Ramsey is in the back room. He's dead. He's got my bullet in his shoulder, but that

79

wasn't what killed him. I came here to pick him up, and walked into trouble. You'll find his partner under that table — and Monk's body behind the bar."

"I'll — kill — you!" Lengo breathed, ignoring Dave's explanation. A naked, blind fury drove him, obscuring all reason. "I'll — be coming — for you —"

"I figured you would," Dave said thinly, and stepped back, letting Lengo go. The marshal's legs buckled, and he fell forward. He lay there, unable to get up, humiliation choking him.

Dave turned away and left him there.

CHAPTER
NINE

The sheriff was in the Café, holding his head between the palms of his hands and staring blankly into his coffee cup, when Dave slid onto the stool next to him. He turned and eyed the big man with a dull regard.

"You get to see Doctor Kleeman?"

"Not yet," Dave replied.

"Where've you been?" The sheriff's voice was suspicious.

"Around. I had a talk with your son, and he told me who owned the mouth organ."

Bill Soltight rubbed his unshaved jaw. "Who?"

"Man name of Zack Miller. Hung out in Barraby's Pool Hall."

"Hung out?" Bill straightened and eyed Dave with closer scrutiny. "What happened? You didn't go into Barraby's looking for Zack?"

Dave shrugged. "Zack's dead," he said evenly. "So's his side-kick, Voss Garrett. And I reckon you could say that Monk Barraby passed away, too."

Sheriff Soltight spun around on his stool. "Whoa!" he rumbled. "You're moving too fast for me, Dave. Tell it to me again — slow."

Dave told him. "Someone beat me to Zack," he summed up. "Just how he killed him puzzles me. But Zack was killed because someone knew I was after him — and he was afraid that Zack would talk. They were waiting for me when I went in — Barraby, Voss and a couple of other gents."

Soltight shook his head slowly and shut his eyes against the pounding behind his eyes. His hangover was killing him.

"Who?" he whispered.

"I don't know," Dave said. He eyed the sheriff coldly, wondering if Soltight was putting on an act. The sheriff could have feigned his hangover and beaten him pool hall.

"Where were you, Bill, after I left the office?"

The sheriff's neck swelled. "Me? You don't think I —" His voice broke with rage. "By Gawd, I ought to take that badge from you and make you eat it!"

"It was a fair question," Dave said coldly. He took Lengo's Colt from his waistband and placed it on the counter in front of the sheriff. "I had to take this away from that fire-breathing town marshal you're partial to," he explained. "I've got a feeling he'll be around for it. When he shows up, ask him how come he was the first man at the door when the shooting took place in Johnny Cruze's room last night? And ask him how he just happened to be waiting across the street when I went into Barraby's place?"

The sheriff's big hand closed over Lengo's Colt. He watched Dave slip from his stool and walk to the door;

he could feel the blood pounding in his ears, and the ache behind his eyes was sharp and real.

"Shot up Barraby's and took Sol's gun away from him!" He spoke in a dazed mutter. He got up and placed a half-dollar on the counter in front of the open-mouthed counterman.

Hangover or no, he had some checking up to do. He had hired a man he didn't know, and the man had taken over in Paydirt in less than three hours!

Doctor Harry Kleeman was a pale blond man over six feet tall, with narrow, sloping shoulders. He was ⌐ ⌐ g a ten-year-old boy for a long gash in his leg, and the smell of carbolic salve was strong in the doctor's treatment room. He looked up with frowning impatience as Dave Chance entered.

"Wait in the other room, please!" he said sharply. Then he noticed the badge on Dave's coat and shrugged. He finished bandaging the boy's leg in weary silence, patted him on the head and let him go.

Alone with Dave, he asked: "What can I do for you?"

"I've come for some information."

"I thought you might," Doctor Kleeman replied. "You don't seem to be in need of medical attention."

"I could use something for a headache," Dave said. "And I think you'll find some birdshot under my hide. But that isn't what I came here for, Doc."

Doctor Kleeman frowned. "Come into the other room." His voice had authority. Dave shrugged and followed him.

"Sit down — on the table." Doctor Kleeman examined the bump just above Dave's temple and muttered something to himself. "Let's get a look at your back. Take your coat off."

Dave felt irritated. "I didn't come here for treatment. I can't afford it."

Doctor Kleeman ignored him. He helped Dave remove his shirt and undershirt and examined Dave's back. "Move your left arm," he directed. He nodded as Dave did so. "I'd better take them out," he muttered. "They're not bothering you now, but they will later."

Dave gritted his teeth as the doctor used the scalpel. "Three of them," Kleeman said, tossing the small lead pellets on the table beside Dave. He finished by taping bandages across Dave's back. "I'll charge it to the county," he said, turning to put away his tools.

Dave dressed. The tall man stood by the window, looking tired. "I usually have better manners," he apologized.

"You look beat," Dave said.

"I am." Kleeman reached inside his coat for a ready-made cigaret. "It's surprising how many assorted ills can plague the population of a mining town. I seem to spend most of my waking hours treating knife cuts, probing for lead slugs, and bandaging cracked heads." He smiled faintly. "You the new sheriff?"

"No. I work for him."

Kleeman rubbed his eyes. "That's right: elections are still three months off. Shows you how little track of time I keep." He frowned. "I don't know the sheriff very well. He and Doctor Sonner are pretty friendly, and I imagine whatever professional services he might need of a doctor he gets from Sonner."

He turned and went to the door as someone knocked. He opened it, stuck his head into the other room and said: "Just a minute, Cy. I'll be right with you. Boils again, eh?" He closed the door and turned to Dave.

"I'm afraid I'm very busy, Deputy —"

"I'll make my business short," Dave said. "First, did you treat a man named Zack Miller for gunshot wounds in his left shoulder?"

The doctor frowned. "I don't recognize the name — and I haven't treated such a wound lately. Why?"

Dave ignored the question. "The second request is harder to put in words. I want to know what kind of medicine smells sweet and can kill quickly."

Doctor Kleeman scratched his head. "Might be a number of drugs," he said shortly. He walked to a glass-door medicine cabinet and took down a bottle. "This lethal medicine — was it taken orally?"

Dave shook his head. "I don't think so."

Kleeman put the small bottle back on the shelf and took down a larger, dark brown one. "This, maybe," he muttered. He pulled the cork and gave Dave a whiff, then jammed the cork back.

Dave nodded. "That's it." He read the label. "Chloroform, eh? Well, thanks, Doc."

"Chloroform's bad stuff to monkey around with," Doctor Kleeman said worriedly. "Doesn't take too many whiffs to put a man to sleep — for good!"

"That's what I figured," Dave replied. "Thanks for the information."

He left Kleeman standing by the medicine chest, looking old and tired. After a few moments Cy coughed loudly in the next room.

Kleeman locked the medicine cabinet and turned. His shoe kicked an envelope that had fallen under the table. He picked it up. It was sealed and had no identification on it.

The deputy must have dropped it, he thought. He slipped it into his pocket and went to the door. "Come in, Cy," he said tiredly.

Dave Chance went directly to the Canyon House. The lead he had uncovered puzzled him. He was quite sure that Zack had been chloroformed to death, but Doctor Sonner seemed hardly the man to do it. Someone else, close enough to the doctor to get into his medicine chest, could have done it.

The desk clerk shook his head at Dave's question. "Mr. Cruze checked out this morning. I believe he's gone back to the mine."

"Did he leave anything for me?"

The desk clerk checked his pigeonholes. "Nothing, Mr. Chance."

Dave stood undecided. He didn't have a thin dime in his pockets, and it irked him. He should have asked Johnny for some money. He didn't want to go to see Sheriff Soltight for an advance against his pay, and though he knew he could charge his meals at the hotel to Johnny's account, he felt handicapped.

He went up to his room and changed and took time to smoke a cigaret. His shoulder was beginning to stiffen. He clenched his fist and made a rotating motion with his arm — in that small, cheerless room he felt an oppressive loneliness.

Paydirt meant trouble — and he didn't want trouble. He'd had enough of it in the past. If he stayed here he'd have to buck Sol Lengo, and he knew he wasn't fast enough for the marshal.

Even Bill Soltight would turn against him eventually when he found out Dave was working for Johnny Cruze.

The thought brought a wry grin to his lips. He had come here to wring ten thousand dollars out of Johnny's hide — and been turned aside by the old line of glib talk. Johnny had dangled an improbable carrot of big money in front of him, and he had taken the bait. For a half-share in the Canyon line, it was now his job to risk his neck to save it.

He got up, suddenly restless and knowing what he had to do. He wouldn't wait until Johnny came back to Paydirt; he'd pay Johnny a visit on Big Lars. He'd settle for five thousand dollars and a full belly.

He didn't run into anyone he knew on his way to the depot. The day had turned gloomy. Thick gray clouds banked the hills, thrusting tendrils over Paydirt. He felt a chill in the air.

The station agent shrugged at his question. "Mr. Cruze left on the ten o'clock train. I think there was some labor trouble up at the mine."

"When does the next train to Big Lars pull out?"

"Only one a day," the agent replied. "Sometimes not every day."

Dave was disappointed. He turned and looked across the tracks to where the Canyon line rails curved toward the narrow gorge a mile away.

"How far by trail to Big Lars?"

The agent raised his eyeshade to study Dave. "About twenty-three miles."

"Can a horse make it?"

"If he's part mule." The man frowned. "You couldn't make it to Big Lars before night. And I wouldn't advise trying that grade after dark." He saw the look on Dave's face and added dryly: "There's the Roost, about twelve miles in. You might make it there before dark."

"The Roost?"

"Used to be a halfway change-over station for Sheriff Soltight's mule train. Now it's a watering point for the railroad. Some old guy name of Holly Jackson acts as caretaker. He'll put you up for the night."

Dave nodded his thanks. He couldn't afford to wait until Johnny returned to Paydirt. He knew Sol Lengo wouldn't let him wait that long. He thought of Bill Soltight and pushed aside his momentary regret. For Bill, too, he was only a means to an end. Bill didn't give a hoot about the Canyon line. But he hated Duke Mason and the crowd at the Golden Nugget, and he saw in Dave a means of stopping Mason.

The badge on his coat weighed little more than an ounce, but it seemed to drag him down now as he turned away from the small depot. Across the tracks was the terminal point of the Santa Fe spur — a man was standing on the low platform and looking down the track. He kept glancing at his watch, and Dave turned to look.

Johnny had told him that the Santa Fe ran a combination freight and passenger train into Paydirt twice a month. This, obviously, was the day the train was due in.

Dave turned and searched the street up from the depot, looking for the sheriff's bulky figure. There was constant movement along the walks, and wagons rumbled through town. He thought he saw Laura Soltight's trim figure cross the street, but he wasn't sure.

A fleeting regret held him. The girl was a misfit in this town. She wanted more than it offered her, and she seemed not the type to lower her standards. Which could mean slow frustration and eventual bitterness, unless she broke free of her father and brother and went East to some bigger city.

He rubbed his bristly jaw with his knuckles, his eyes suddenly thoughtful. He had spent two years looking for Johnny Cruze — two years of rootless existence. Five thousand dollars could carry him a long way. But where was he headed?

He shrugged, angry with himself for his indecision. Whatever was in store for him, he would not find it in Paydirt.

He walked back to the stables where he had left his horse. By day Paydirt was a squalid, hurrying town with an air of frustrated activity. The more respectable business establishments, the small combination courthouse and Sunday church, the stone bank and the print shop which put out a weekly one-page newspaper were on the south side of the river.

The section which had sprung up across the river, consisting mostly of rickety, green-board structures and tents and cribs catering to human vices, had been nicknamed by some impious soul, "The Holy Acre."

By day it was a quiet, miserable section made more repelling by the dismal overcast.

Dave saddled his big roan, showed the reluctant stableman his badge and told him to charge the animal's keep to the sheriff's office. The man did not feel physically inclined to argue the point, but his skepticism was plain in his eyes.

Riding out to the main street, Dave turned toward the sheriff's office. The door was not locked, but the sheriff was out.

Dave hesitated only a moment. He found a pencil in the sheriff's desk and wrote on the back of a recent dodger: *Have gone up to the mines. See you in a couple of days.*

He signed it, propped it against the pigeonholes on the desk and left. It was beginning to drizzle as he entered the dark cut of the canyon and disappeared from the sight of Paydirt.

CHAPTER
TEN

Doctor Kleeman was closing up for a late lunch when Sheriff Soltight came in. The doctor nodded a curt greeting.

"I was," he said tiredly, "just about to stop by your office, Sheriff. Just a minute and I'll get it for you."

"Get what?"

"A letter your deputy dropped in my office," Doctor Kleeman said.

Bill Soltight frowned. His head ached dully behind his eyes, and his stomach was still queasy. He sat down on one of the straight-backed chairs in the waiting room.

"Was Dave in here?"

Kleeman had stepped into the next room. His voice came back through the open door. "Yes, about fifteen minutes ago. He had a lump the size of a pigeon egg over his right ear, and some birdshot in him." Kleeman appeared in the doorway with the envelope. "I treated him. He said he was broke, and I told him I'd charge it to the county —"

"Generous of you," Bill muttered. He knew Doctor Kleeman didn't like him, and he always felt slightly old and incapable in his presence. "I reckon we can stand the bill."

Doctor Kleeman shrugged, his manner keeping a cool barrier between them. "This fell out of his coat pocket," he said, holding out the envelope. "I'm sure he'll want it."

Bill took it and slid it into his pocket. "Did he come to you for medical attention?"

"Not primarily," Kleeman answered. "In fact, it was my idea to treat him. Actually, he came to me for some information."

Soltight stood up. The close odors from the other room turned his stomach. "What was he after?"

"He wanted to know if I had treated a man named Zack Miller for a shoulder wound recently. And — oh, yes, he seemed interested in chloroform."

"What?"

"Chloroform. He was quite interested in its properties." Kleeman's voice took on a sarcastic edge. "You say he works for you?"

Soltight took a grip on his sadly frayed temper. "Temporarily. My son is laid up and —"

"Oh?"

"Dave will be working for me just until Rick is back on his feet," Bill said. "If it's worrying you, I'll pay his bill."

"I feel it's worrying you," Kleeman said coldly. "Did you want to see me about something else?"

"Not medically," Bill growled angrily. He turned and left the waiting room, feeling like a small boy who had

92

just been chided for some prank. The damp breeze braced him somewhat, steadied his stomach.

He knew Laura was waiting dinner for him, but he felt little inclination for food. He stopped by the hotel and learned that Dave Chance had left. The clerk thought he had gone to the depot.

At the depot, he was told by the Canyon line agent that Dave had asked about a train to Big Lars and had settled for the long ride up the narrow, treacherous trail.

Bill stood on the platform, a scowl on his face. The Santa Fe train was coming into sight around the far bend, up from the sloping flatlands southeast of Paydirt. Its yellow headlight stabbed through the gray afternoon.

Bill went back to his office. He found Dave's note on his desk and hurled it aside. Then he remembered the envelope Doctor Kleeman had given him, and curiosity was an easy victor over his scruples.

He opened the envelope and read the partnership agreement Johnny Cruze had signed, making Dave Chance half-owner of the Devil's Canyon Railroad.

When Sol Lengo walked in on Bill Soltight a half-hour later, the sheriff was standing by the window, head hunched forward, hands thrust deep inside his pockets. He looked like a man who had sucked on a lemon. His mouth was drawn in, and his bloodshot eyes had an ugly look.

Sol slammed the door behind him and swung around to face Bill. The sheriff was in a grim mood, but Sol had never bothered about anyone else's feelings. His came out thick, breaking a little with the intensity behind it.

"I'll take my gun, Bill! Then I'm going to kill him!"

Soltight turned and walked to the desk without saying a word. He pulled open a drawer and placed Lengo's Colt on the desk. Then he cocked his head to one side and looked at Sol, as though seeing the man for the first time.

Lengo checked his Colt and slid it into his holster. His face was still tinged with yellow, and he seemed to have some difficulty drawing a deep breath.

"You gave him a badge, Bill!" he snarled. "Gave him a legal excuse for what he did —"

"What did he do. Sol?" Bill's voice was unusually gentle.

Sol let his gaze rest on the sheriff's face. The tone of Bill's voice held something he couldn't quite understand, and it puzzled him, for he took Bill as a matter of course.

"Busted up Barraby's!" he said grimly. "Crossed the river first thing this morning and went into Barraby's on the thin excuse he was looking for someone connected with Ramsey's killing."

"Maybe he was," Bill said coldly. "Maybe Dave knew something —"

Sol put the palms of his hands on the desk top and leaned toward the sheriff. "He wanted an excuse to throw his weight around across the river. He knew that badge you gave him would cover him."

"How'd he do it?"

Bill's question, inserted casually, checked Lengo's tirade. He turned, his lips bloodlessly tight against his strong teeth. "Do what?"

"Take your gun away from you?"

Lengo's eyes glared. He couldn't keep humiliation from flooding his face.

"Surprised me as I came running into Barraby's." His voice drew thin as a knife edge. "I never liked him, Bill. I don't trust him. But for what he did today, I'm going to kill him!"

Bill shook his head. "Bring him in, Sol."

Sol straightened, a wicked glint in his eyes. "I'll bring him in! Head down, across the front of my saddle!"

Soltight's face was like stone. He had been doing a lot of thinking in the interval since he had opened Dave's letter and Sol had walked in. It was not the first time in his life he had looked himself over, but he had done a good job of it this time.

He had been small time all of his life. Yet he had been a man of ambition — he had wanted more for himself and his family than the dubious security of a sheriff's pay. He was not a politician and knew his chances of being elected to higher office were slim.

Nor was he a good businessman. The mule train was the third venture he had failed in. Defeat, he thought sourly, has a habit of sitting hard on a man's shoulders, turning him sour.

So he had resented Johnny Cruze's coming to Paydirt at the moment when the Devil's Canyon Railroad had gone broke. Still, he had reflected, Johnny Cruze had the devil's own gift of speech, to have talked

Severson and Fillmore into selling for a third of the amount they might have received if they had held out just a little longer.

Johnny Cruze he had sized up as a lightweight, and he had not changed his mind about him. Money didn't change what was inside a man. And he didn't want Johnny calling on Laura. He had a great deal of respect for his daughter's judgment, but Laura was at the age when a certain anxiety set in. A girl of twenty-four who is still unmarried, he reflected, begins to feel the pressure of time. And it was possible that Johnny Cruze, with his smooth line of talk, could make an impression on her.

Between Johnny and Sol Lengo, he had always leaned toward this harder, more violent man.

Now he said again, slowly and deliberately, "Bring him in, Sol, alive!"

Sol sneered. "He's my problem, Bill; not yours."

Soltight searched Lengo's hard face. "Why, Sol?" he asked abruptly. "Because he took your gun away from you?"

"Because I don't like anything about him," Sol shot back.

"That ain't enough, Sol. He's a sworn officer of the law. He had a right to go into Barraby's. And if there was any shooting —"

"He killed three men!" Sol cut in harshly. "Bill, there ain't two kinds of law in Paydirt. The citizens across the river deserve the same protection as the do-gooders on this side. And no stranger, even if he is wearing your badge, can walk into a place like Barraby's and start shooting up the place without answering to me!"

Bill sucked in a harsh breath. "Sol," he grated, shaking a thick finger across the desk, "don't tell me about law and justice! And don't try to put Monk and that crew across the river on a level with most of the citizens on this side. Don't make me swallow that!"

"If the bite's too big, spit it out!" Sol snarled. "But I'll remind you, seeing as how you seem to have forgotten, that running this town is my business!"

Bill checked himself. He nodded slowly. "Maybe running it is the right way to put it," he breathed. "All right, Sol. I've never stuck my nose into your business. I've been on your side all along, and you know it. You've got a tough job on that side of the river."

"I've never complained."

Bill nodded, but his lips took on a sour twist. "Maybe because it isn't so tough, after all, eh, Sol? Looking back now, you spend a lot of time in Duke's place. And though there's been rough stuff in Barraby's before, somehow you never jailed anyone, or got into trouble in Monk's place yourself. Sure, if a drunk gets out of line on this side of the river, he's buffaloed and shoved into jail. And there was another stranger who came to town about a month ago, wasn't it? He got into trouble in Duke's place, I recall. Claimed he was being cheated. You killed him, Sol, didn't you?"

"I tried to stop him from making trouble, and he drew on me!" Sol snarled.

"Sure. It was self-defense." Bill's mouth was harsh. "But it's only people like that stranger and drunks on this side of the river that you tangle with. Never Duke's men or Barraby's tough crowd."

"What are you getting at, Bill?" Sol's voice was mean. "Well, spit it out!"

Bill's big hands clenched. "For the first time I'm asking a few questions I should have asked before. What's between you and that bunch across the river? A rake-off?"

"What if there is?"

Bill's breath escaped in a small sigh. "It isn't new," he muttered. "It's been done before, and by men with more of a reputation. Even Wyatt Earp's got a good thing going in Dodge City —"

"Then why blame me?"

"I'm not blaming you. But it makes you stand just a little crooked, Sol. Changes my picture of you."

Sol rubbed the back of his hand across his mouth. "I never tried to give you a different picture, Bill."

"No, you haven't," the sheriff admitted. His voice was heavy with an odd disappointment. "It was me. I was looking for something in you I thought I once had. A tough lawman, but honest. I wanted that, Sol, because of Laura."

Sol laughed. It was a thin and wicked laughter. "You built too high a fence around her, Bill. I wasn't interested."

Soltight's face darkened. "Maybe —" he said bleakly.

"But I'm a better man for her than Johnny Cruze," Sol stated flatly. "And I may just decide to jump that fence —"

"Try it and I'll kill you!"

Sol came up on his toes, his hand on his gun butt. "You're old, Bill. Past your time. Don't go making threats you can't back up!"

"Stay away from my daughter!" Bill said thickly.

Lengo laughed. The echo of his insolence came back to Bill after the marshal had gone, twisting into him like a knife blade.

He sat down slowly, his eyes on the dirty window, not seeing what lay beyond. His big hand closed over Dave's envelope, and unconsciously he crumpled it between his fingers . . .

CHAPTER
ELEVEN

Leaving the cigar store on Gold Street, Doctor Sonner saw Dave Chance come out of the sheriff's office, step into the saddle of a big roan waiting at the rack, and ride for the Canyon trail. He stopped on the edge of the walk to light a cigar and watched the big deputy disappear into the gloom of the gorge.

He was an asthmatic, and he had spent most of the morning in bed in his cramped, untidy quarters behind his office. At such a time smoking did him little good, but he felt the need of a calming cigar.

Dave bothered him. The big man's comings and goings had a purpose he mistrusted. He decided to see the sheriff and learn what was taking Dave up the trail to Big Lars. Obviously it was urgent, or the deputy would have waited to make the trip by train.

The sheriff was not in his office. Sonner read the notice Dave had propped on the desk, but did not tamper with it. He went out and walked slowly back toward the hotel, and was on the verge of crossing the river to find Lengo when he saw Bill Soltight go into Doctor Kleeman's office.

The day had turned dismal. He felt an attack coming on, and he steadied himself against it. But curiosity turned him into a sloppy lunchroom frequented by stamp mill workers on the night shift. A few of them were clustered around a rickety table in the corner, drinking weak coffee.

Doctor Sonner took a seat near the window. The hot coffee helped a little, but his eyes watered, and he felt irritable and jumpy.

The sheriff passed by a few minutes later, a big, angry-looking man with his thoughts churning over some problem of his own. Doctor Sonner paid for his coffee and went out.

He intercepted Doctor Kleeman on his way to dinner, ignored the man's unfriendliness, and found out what he wanted to know. Doctor Kleeman obviously didn't give a hoot about what went on in the sheriff's office.

Sonner walked slowly back to his own office. He waited a few moments, hoping to see Sol Lengo show up, but his breathing was becoming more difficult. He turned into his office, where he put a pan of water on the stove. When it began to steam, he bent over it, sucking in painful gasps of air.

He was feeling a little better when he walked slowly to the door and looked out. He decided he had to see Sol Lengo and turned up the street to the cubbyhole where Lengo had his office. The marshal was out. Disappointed, Sonner backtracked to his own office and turned the corner in time to see Lengo step out of the sheriff's office.

The doctor waited on the walk until the marshal strode by; he jerked his head significantly, and Lengo nodded curtly.

Doctor Sonner went back to his office, locked the front door, and waited in the back room where he lived.

Ten minutes later Lengo came in by way of the alley. He opened the back door without knocking, closed it behind him and stood in the center of Sonner's room, a lean, dangerous man with an ugly look in his yellow-gray eyes.

"He shot his way out of Barraby's," he said abruptly.

Doctor Sonner nodded. "I heard about it." His eyes behind his glasses were a bright blue. "I told you he was no fool. He's no stranger drifting through Paydirt. He came here for a reason —"

"Johnny Cruze sent for him!" Lengo cut in bitterly. "He must have. He went to see Johnny last night, after he killed Jules. Sure he killed Jules!" the marshal snapped. "I got there too late to —"

"I know," Sonner interrupted. "What happened at Barraby's?"

Lengo told him. "I underrated him, Doc. Figured him to be a big clumsy jasper with a hard right hand. I saw him draw against Duke. It was fast — but not that fast. And he almost missed Duke —"

"You don't win bets with near misses," Doc reminded him coldly.

"No. That's why I put my bets on sure things," Lengo said. "I'm going to kill him!"

Doc smiled faintly. "Why do you say Johnny Cruze sent for him?"

"Because of last night. I did some checking. He's been charging his meals at the hotel to Cruze."

"Does Bill know?"

"I don't think so. I don't give a hoot, either. If Bill gets in our way, I'll kill him, too."

"Don't worry about the sheriff," Sonner said quickly. "I'll handle him."

"What about Dave Chance?"

Doc Sonner turned and sat down on his bed. He made a gesture of impatience. "I just saw him head for the Canyon trail a little more than a half-hour ago. He left a note for Bill saying he was going up to Big Lars and would be gone for a couple of days."

Lengo frowned. "Why would he do that?"

"I can make a guess," Doc Sonner said quietly. "He must have caught a whiff of chloroform in Barraby's back room. He checked with Doctor Kleeman — I know, because I had a little talk with my colleague — and asked Kleeman what chloroform smelled like. He asked if Kleeman had treated Zack for a shoulder wound recently."

"He's no fool," Lengo said grudgingly. "He's moving faster than Bill Soltight's moved in six months."

"He had a lucky break," Doc conceded. "And he's big, but not dumb. Once he starts putting two and two together —"

"You'll hang!" Lengo said thinly.

"You'll hang with me!" Sonner snapped, nettled by Sol's tone. Then he made a pacifying gesture. "It doesn't have to be that way at all. I've got Bill sold on the idea Johnny Cruze froze him out of the Devil's Canyon Railroad partnership. He'll listen to anything I have to say about Johnny — and about Dave Chance."

Sol gritted his teeth in frustration. "One more payroll, and Cruze would have folded. We'd have been able to pick up the Devil's Canyon Railroad for as little as he bought it for — and pay for it with the money we stole from him!"

"We got a bad break when Zack and Voss let Ramsey get away from them," Sonner muttered, "before you showed up. Still, if they had caught up with Irving before he reached the creek —"

"Second guessing ain't gonna change anything," Sol growled.

Sonner got up, walked to his small back window and looked out into the littered alley. He spoke to the window, but the marshal heard his every word distinctly.

"Dave Chance is riding right now on one of the most dangerous trails in the Territory. He doesn't know anything about it. My guess, Sol, is that he'll put up tonight at the Roost." He turned and eyed the marshal. "You want to get back at him for what happened at Barraby's?"

Lengo nodded, his eyes cold and remote, looking ahead.

"Take Manny with you," Doc advised. "This is one play we've got to make sure of. Whatever happens, don't let Dave Chance come back to Paydirt."

"What about the sheriff?"

"I'll handle Bill," Sonner said impatiently.

Lengo rubbed his sore stomach. "All right, Doc — I'll take care of Chance . . ."

CHAPTER
TWELVE

The trail to Big Lars was a tortuous climb that brought out the sweat on the big roan's sleek hide. The Canyon line rails followed the old mule trail most of the way. But there were times when the iron road branched off and crossed narrow chasms on trestle bridges that seemed flimsy and unsafe against the bold jagged cliffs rising above them.

At one place the railroad tunneled through two hundred feet of solid granite; at other points it hung a thousand feet above the white water of Devil's Creek.

It had taken money, imagination and engineering know-how to build this short haul railroad, and with the slowly passing miles respect came to Dave Chance for the men who had conceived and carried out the building of the road.

They had taken every natural advantage to keep the grade within operating limits, but Dave guessed that even the powerful Mallet engine probably crawled at no more than a snail's pace up the winding road.

It grew colder as he climbed higher into the hills. Rain clouds brushed the high slopes, and a wet mist clung to him. He moved in a world constricted and hemmed in by giant pine slopes and sometimes sheer gray rock faces from which water seeped to stain them the color of rust.

He found no place along that narrow trail where anything larger than a ground hog might hide. Finally he came around one more bend, and the steep slope pulled away from him, leaving a clearing among the hills. The slope behind the clearing was gentler, rising and losing itself in the clouds.

The Roost flanked the mule trail which parted from the rails here, cutting across the slope toward a break in the cliffs beyond. It was a story-and-a-half wooden building with a steep gable roof and a covered veranda, and coming up to it, Dave saw that it had been built on the edge of a ravine from which came the sound of rushing water.

He pulled up, feeling the dampness get at him and lower his spirits. His shoulder had stiffened, and the slight pain over his ear was a faint reminder of the morning.

He had expected more. The Roost seemed untenanted, an ugly unpainted structure slowly falling into disrepair. Beyond it Dave saw an old corral, more neglected than the house, and closer, a shed with a steep slanting roof designed, like that of the house, to shed snow.

The rails of the Canyon line diverged at this clearing and kept close to Devil's Creek, out of sight and barely heard now below the rim of the trail. A water tank on rickety wooden stilts flanked the roadbed, fed by a two-inch pipe which came down from the higher slopes.

Dave shook himself. It was a cheerless welcome, and he was sorry now that he had decided to ride up to Big Lars to see Johnny. He could have waited a day or two more.

He dismounted and stood against the roan and surveyed the house again. His legs felt stiff.

Then he saw a big dog staring at him from the far corner of the building. It was a shaggy-haired, long-nosed tan dog with enough of the collie in him to make the strain stand out. His coat was wet, and he sniffed the air, eyeing Dave steadily. He was big enough, Dave thought, to give him trouble if he was mean.

The mist was beginning to turn into a fine rain. Behind Dave the roan shook his head and whinnied questioningly. Dave nodded. "I'll take care of you, boy," he told the animal. "Shed looks like it might have some dry spots."

The dog watched him. When Dave casually let his hand touch the butt of his gun, the animal jumped backward and disappeared.

Dave grinned. The animal knew what a gun meant.

He brought the roan into the barn. It turned out to be not much of a shelter. He could see through broken boards, and it was beginning to leak through the roof in several places.

Dave found an area that seemed dry, stripped his saddle from the roan and tied him to a post. There was some old hay in a corner which he brought back to the animal.

"Poor pickings, feller," he said sympathetically, running a hand over the roan's wet muzzle. "But you can stand it for a day. You've been getting fat and sassy back in town —"

He heard a soft scuffling behind him and whirled. The muzzle of the dog disappeared from the doorway. A cold prickle raised the short hair on Dave's neck. He put his hand on his Colt butt.

The rain sifted across his face as he stepped out. Except for the dog, there seemed to be no one about. He crossed the yard at a run and had his foot on the first rotted step when a voice said from the darkness above him: "You aiming to stay the night?"

Dave waited on the first step. He heard the dog sniff behind him, somewhere in the fading, dismal day. But he couldn't make out the owner of the voice, though he could see that the door was open and someone was standing just inside.

"Step out where I can see you, Jackson," he said, "and I'll tell you."

The man in the doorway sniffed as though he had a cold. "How'd you know my name?"

"Station agent down at Paydirt told me a man named Holly Jackson was up here and could put me up for the night."

The man in the doorway stepped out onto the porch. There was enough daylight for Dave to make out a long-shanked, bony man in greasy buckskins. His hair was long and shaggy and pepper-gray, and he was holding a big bore shotgun as if it were a toy.

In the bad light he didn't look old, but his cracked voice was an index to his age. "Be a dollar the night. Meals extra."

Dave shrugged. The rain was seeping down his neck. "Reasonable enough," he muttered. "Let's go inside."

Jackson didn't move. "Hard money, mister. Not that paper folks down in Paydirt hand out."

Dave said grimly: "You'll have to wait to get paid. At the moment I'm flat broke."

Holly Jackson looked him over with diminished respect. "No money?" He was disappointed. Then his face cracked in quick anticipation. "Got whiskey, mebbe?"

Dave shook his head.

Holly grew angry. "What are you doing on this trail with no money?"

"I'm going up to Big Lars. On business." Dave's voice was impatient. "I'll see that you get paid."

Jackson wasn't convinced. "How?"

Dave reached for the envelope he thought he had tucked away in his coat pocket. He didn't find it. He tried his other pockets, and then he dropped his hand and stood there, the rain sifting down his collar. He had dropped the partnership agreement somewhere. Thinking back, he knew it must have been when he had taken off his coat in Doctor Kleeman's office.

It was too late to turn back for it now. Doctor Kleeman would keep it for him, or turn it over to Bill Soltight.

Jackson's slow skeptical voice interrupted his thoughts. "Wa-al, feller?"

"Reckon I can't move it to you," Dave said. He started to turn away. "Mind if I sleep in the barn?"

"Heck, you kin come inside," the caretaker said. He chuckled with an odd sense of humor. "Just wanted to see how you'd take it. Some jaspers without a red cent in their jeans talk big . . ."

Dave said: "Much obliged, Jackson," and went up the stairs.

Lights pushed back the gloom inside the house as the old man lighted an oil lamp. In the yellow glare, he seemed even more gaunt and bony, and in his buckskins he was like a relic of the country's past. His neck skin hung in folds, and his cheekbones were sharply prominent.

"Got a mess of rabbit stew cooking in the kitchen," he said. "Hungry?"

" 'll eat anything," Dave said. He unbuttoned his coat and took a notch in his belt and watched Jackson walk the length of the room and open a door which led out onto a flying balcony overhanging the ravine. There was water below, for Jackson hauled up a bucket of water, using a pulley arrangement bolted into a beam which extended beyond the balcony.

"I'll make some fresh coffee," he said, walking back with the oak bucket. "Make yourself at home, Mister —"

"Dave Chance," Dave said.

"Fire'll help you dry out, Dave," Jackson said. "Wood in the box in the corner — over there. More in the shed just back of the house."

He disappeared into the kitchen. Dave walked over to the big stone fireplace and got a fire started. He took off his wet coat, hung it over the back of a rickety chair and set it near the blaze. Then he took a good look around.

The Roost was like some drafty barn, with an unfinished, exposed beam ceiling and only two windows, one facing the yard, the other at the back of the house. Both windows were small, but the glass was intact.

Narrow wooden stairs, anchored to the east wall, went up and disappeared into a plank door set flush at the head of them. Dave guessed that whatever sleeping quarters the place provided lay beyond that door.

Several long plank trestle tables and accompanying benches were probably a leftover from the time when the Roost was a way station for travelers on the railroad on their way up to the mines.

There were two overhead lamps, but Holly had lighted only the one nearest the door. It provided light enough for the bench almost directly under it, but scarcely penetrated the shadows at the far end of the room.

The rain was beginning to drum softly against the roof of the house. Dave massaged his fingers. The fire flickered cheerfully, and the warmth that began to creep into him lifted his spirits. He had told Jackson he was hungry out of politeness; now he was beginning to feel ravenous.

Jackson's voice, seemingly anticipating him, came through the thin partition separating them. "Be ready in a minute, Dave."

Dave walked to the balcony where Jackson had hauled in his water. He stepped out and felt the floor under him quiver at his weight. Below him, in the darkness, he could hear the rush of water — he couldn't tell how far down it was.

A low, sturdy railing enclosed the balcony. Beyond it was nothing, and then a dark mountainous mass loomed up against the drizzly sky. He could barely make it out, but he could feel its presence, rising dark and massive beyond the ravine.

He turned back into the long room as Jackson came out of the kitchen with a couple of cracked, glazed plates and set them down on the table under the light.

"Chow's on," he called, and went back into the kitchen for other utensils.

Dave ate in silence. The other man was not talkative, although he seemed glad to have Dave's company. Within that room, warmed by the blazing fire, Dave could still feel the mountains towering over them, and it gave him a closed-in feeling he didn't like.

When Jackson brought in the coffee, Dave sat back and rolled a cigaret. He watched the old man slop coffee from his mug into a saucer and blow on it.

"Must get pretty lonely up here," Dave made conversation.

The caretaker sucked at his coffee. "Got company," he mumbled. "Got Jake."

Dave looked toward the kitchen.

"My dog," Holly Jackson explained. He wiped his mouth with the back of his hand. "Jake and me don't need anybody."

Dave was silent for a long while, listening to the rain. Then, "How long have you been up here?"

"Fifteen years."

"Before the railroad?"

"Before the sheriff and his mule train." Jackson finished his coffee. "Saw a badge on yore coat. You the new deppity?"

Dave nodded. "Temporary job, though. Just until the sheriff's boy gets back on his feet."

The caretaker snorted softly as he dug into the stew for a second helping. "Bill's boy run into a bullet?"

"Ran into too many fists," Dave said dryly. He explained briefly. "Doc Sonner thinks Rick will be laid up for at least a week —"

He stopped and turned to watch the big dog pad softly in from the kitchen and settle by the fire.

Jackson indicated the pot. "There's more," he invited.

Dave declined politely. Jackson cooked with a liberal hand on the salt and pepper and some other strange ingredients not palatable to Dave. But he did pour himself another cup of coffee.

"How much farther to the mines?"

Holly Jackson shrugged.

" 'Bout five miles, straight over Grayback." He jerked a thumb over his shoulder, toward the balcony.

"By trail?"

"Not for a horse," Jackson answered. "Not even a mule —"

Dave settled back. "How far by trail?"

"Twelve miles." Jackson pushed his plate aside. "Yo're the first man I've seen ride up here in six months."

"Rough trail," Dave said.

"Gets worse from here," the caretaker said cheerfully.

He turned quickly as the dog growled. The animal had come to its feet and was staring at the closed door, ears cocked forward.

Holly moved faster than Dave had thought he could. He was on his feet and scooping up the shotgun he had placed beside the door before Dave rose. Jackson stepped on the bench table, turned the light down and waited by the door.

A rider was coming toward the house. Dave heard him clearly. He dismounted and came up the steps and opened the door and stood puzzled, eyeing Holly and Dave by the table.

He was a short, thick man, younger than Dave. An Army poncho covered him. He looked at the gun in Holly's hand, and his teeth showed white against his dark face.

"It's me," he said. "Manuel Cardoza."

Holly Jackson obviously knew the man. But he seemed puzzled. He set the shotgun down against the wall and closed the door behind the new arrival. "You come alone, Manny?"

The other nodded. "Lost my shirt gambling in town. Going back to work —" He glanced at Dave and nodded pleasantly. "Coffee smells good. I'll join you soon's I take this off."

Holly licked his lips. He had changed with Manny's arrival; he seemed uncertain of himself. "I'll set another plate," he said, and disappeared into the kitchen.

Manny Cardoza walked to the fire and looked down at Dave's coat draped over the chair. He took his poncho off and dropped it carelessly. Turning, Dave saw that he wore a gun belt, a tool not usually considered necessary by miners.

The dog was still standing, staring toward the door. A low questioning sound vibrated in his throat.

Dave moved slowly back from the table, away from the light. Manny watched him. The dog paced to the door and waited, as if he knew someone was outside in the dark wet night.

Holly Jackson was strangely quiet in the kitchen. Dave's uneasiness grew. He moved back slowly, his eyes on Manny and the kitchen door. He was headed for the small balcony overhanging the ravine, the darkest place in the room.

Manny grew restless. "*Señor* — do not allow me to interfere with your supper."

"I'm through," Dave said. The cigaret had gone dead between his lips, and he reached toward his pocket, without thinking, for a match.

Manny was pitched too high. He reacted to Dave's move, jerked his knife from its sheath at the back of his neck and threw it.

Dave ducked. The blade went past him, out over the railing. He drew and got in a quick snap shot, and

115

Manny spun around and tripped over the hearth. He fell across the burning logs, almost smothering the fire.

Dave's next shot, taken with more care, smashed the lamp. There was a bluish flare-up just before the room darkened, and then a reddish flare from the kitchen gave him a brief glimpse of Sol Lengo's hard, tight face. The bullet from Sol's gun was close.

Dave stepped out to the balcony. From the far end of the room he heard Holly's thin, excited voice command: "Get him, Jake!"

The dog's pads make a soft drumming on the floor boards as he came for Dave. It was almost completely dark in the room, but a flicker of flame appeared beside Manny's body. It provided just enough light for Dave to see the big dog as he came up in a silent leap for Dave's throat.

Dave fired hastily and knew he had hit the animal. It did not stop him. The dog landed on his chest, and he felt the animal's jaws close down on his shoulder as he fell backward. The railing stopped him for a brief instant; then he went over it in a backward fall.

The dog fell with him.

CHAPTER
THIRTEEN

The wooden match flickered in the cold draft and went out. Holly cursed as he fumbled in his pockets for another.

Sol Lengo said tightly: "Give me a hand with Manny. He's beginning to smell like cooked meat."

Holly scraped his second match and lighted the candle in his hand. He set the small flame down on the table, anchoring it in a small pool of hot tallow drippings. Then he turned and helped Sol drag Manny out of the fire-place.

The candle flickered dangerously, casting their long shadows in a sinuous dance over the stone fireplace. Holly's nose wrinkled. "I'll get the kitchen light," he excused himself, and went out of the room.

Sol turned Manny over and grimaced at the dead man's face. He straightened and moved away from the body, and Holly came in, carrying a glass-based kerosene lamp which he placed on the table beside the candle. He looked down at the broken glass of the overhead lamp in disgust.

The marshal walked out to the balcony. The rain slanted under the overhang and wet him. He looked down into the darkness, trying to make out something below. He vaguely saw what appeared to be a white froth; nothing more. The roar of the stream was a steady, fretting sound.

From inside the room behind him, Holly said: "I sure hate to lose Jake.

The marshal looked down into the ravine a moment longer. Then he turned and walked back to what was left of the man who had ridden up there with him.

"I hate to lose Manny, too," he muttered.

Holly said practically: "The weather won't hurt him none. Let's get him out into the wood shed — I'll bury him tomorrow."

They came back into the house, and Holly rebuilt the fire. Sol stood before it, holding his hands out to the flames. "I told Manny to wait," he said, "keep his attention. I wanted him, Holly — wanted him bad!"

Holly sucked in his lips over stubby teeth. "He said he worked for Bill Soltight —"

"Bill's an old fool!" Sol growled. "He wanted to get back at Duke for the beating his boy took the other night. Packy picked a fight with the kid over one of Duke's girls, and Duke saw a chance to make a big thing out of it. Built a ring inside the Golden Nugget and took the bunch of suckers from across the river who bet on Rick Soltight —"

"Much of a fight?"

"The kid was willing," Sol admitted. "I give him that much. Packy cut him to pieces."

"How'd this big feller, Dave, get mixed up in it?"

Sol told him. "Far as Bill was concerned, it was the only good thing that happened that night, so he offered

Chance a badge." Sol shrugged. "He didn't come to town by chance, Holly. Johnny Cruze sent for him. He came into town packing Irv Ramsey across his saddle."

Holly looked worried. "Sol, I did my job. I packed Ramsey on my mule over Grayback and down to the shack where Zack and Voss were waiting. I did my job, Sol."

"Nobody's blaming you," Sol said. "Ramsey didn't talk."

Holly was shaking his head. "Just the same, if the sheriff starts asking questions —"

"Doc Sonner'll handle Bill!" Sol snapped. He turned away from the fire. "I packed some whiskey in my saddlebag. Get some coffee. I'll lace mine."

Holly rubbed his hands. "Waste of good whiskey," he sniffed.

The rain was worse in the morning. Sol was in a bad temper. He walked out to the balcony and peered down at the water below, half hidden by mist. The stream came rushing down from the higher slopes, cutting through a narrow rocky gorge, and made a small pool before spilling over rocks farther on.

Holly came up to join him. "Might take a week to find what happened to him," he said.

"I have to get back," Sol said. "But you go down and make sure, soon as the rain lets up. I've got to know."

Holly shrugged. "What do I tell the sheriff if he comes nosing around? He'll find the deppity's roan —"

"Not if you get rid of him," Sol said grimly. "Dave rode up to Big Lars. That's what you'll tell him."

They went back into the big room. Sol cleaned his Colt while Holly got breakfast. He waited with growing irritation until mid-morning, when the rain slackened a little.

"I'm riding back," he told Holly. "Remember what I told you." He went to the barn, where he saddled and mounted, draping his poncho around him. Holly was on the porch, watching, as he rode by.

"Get rid of Manny's cayuse, too," the marshal ordered. "I'll get you another dog . . ."

The threatening rain didn't come to Paydirt. The clouds hung thick and ominous over the peaks, and Sheriff Soltight, peering through his window, knew it was raining in the mountains.

Behind him the kitchen clock banged out eight tinny strokes. He stared glumly at the flower bed below the window. He felt tired and out of sorts, and he knew it was more than the let-down which came after a drunk. He had been lifted too high by the thought of beating Duke Mason and his crowd; he had expected too much of a man he had not known at all.

The smell of crisp bacon mingled with that of freshly brewed coffee. Usually he ate breakfast; Laura determinedly insisted. But he wasn't hungry this morning, and Laura had not pressed him.

He turned and reached for his gun belt hanging on a peg by the door. He was only half listening to Rick arguing with Laura; it was a morning occurrence, like biscuits and coffee and eggs, and it had no malice in it. They were in the kitchen, just off the parlor, and Rick

120

was making a nuisance of himself, complaining he was not an invalid and didn't want to be treated like one.

Rick looked worse this morning than on the night of the fight. The bruises had turned blue and lemon yellow, and the lump over his right eye hung like a wen, partially obscuring his vision. His lips were still puffed, and he talked as though he had a potato in his mouth.

But he was an amiable sort with an ingrained good nature, and it irked him to stay indoors. Laura's sisterly voice was ordering him to eat his eggs and to quit complaining. Bill grinned faintly. Laura could handle Rick better than he could.

He was at the door when Laura called to him. He waited for her to join him.

"Early, isn't it?" Her voice indicated she had something on her mind. "Is there something urgent at the office?"

Bill tried to avoid what was coming. "Better off at the office than here, listening to Rick bellyache. I'll be back for dinner."

"I heard some talk last night," she headed him off, "at the store. Meg asked me later if it was true."

"I don't know what you're talking about," her father said brusquely. He pointed to the kitchen. "I think Rick wants more coffee."

"He can get his own coffee!" she snapped. "And don't try to put me off. You know what I mean: about Dave being matched with that professional fighter of Duke's — Packy Shane. Is there any truth in it?"

Sheriff Soltight shrugged. "I've heard rumors. But no one has approached me." He grinned crookedly. "And to my knowledge, no one has asked Dave, either."

Laura frowned. "But is there any truth to it?"

"If Duke thinks he can make a fast dollar on it, there is," her father said bluntly.

"But Shane's a professional!" she cried. "The way he beat Rick —"

"Dave Chance isn't Rick," Bill cut in coldly. He felt resentful and knew why. *It had to come some day*, he thought. And now, faced with it, he felt inadequate. Against Johnny Cruze, he could put up a stand. He didn't like Johnny. But he had liked Dave —

"No, he isn't," Laura answered. "But does that make it less cruel? To put on a show, just so Duke can bet on his fighter?" She made an angry gesture of distance. "The Romans did it two thousand years ago. Have we progressed so little?"

"Why are you so interested?" He stood before her now, asking.

"In Dave?"

He nodded.

"Maybe because he's the first man I've met who looked at me as though I were a person. A woman, yes — but a person, too." She smiled faintly. "It's important, Father."

He was puzzled. "Have I treated you so badly?"

She shook her head. "It's just that to you I'm your daughter. To Rick I'm his sister. And —"

"Johnny Cruze?" he growled. "How does he look at you?"

She colored. "He's been a gentleman," she answered. "But I've always had the feeling that to Johnny I'm some sort of means to an end; something he wants more than me. He's sure of himself with women, more confident than Dave is. But Johnny doesn't need anyone."

"And Dave does?"

She smiled. "I think so."

Bill shook his head. He felt the anger deep within him twist up through his bowels. "Dave doesn't need anybody, Laura. He knows what he came here for — and he's got it!"

She stepped back, searching his face. "What did he come here for?"

"Money!" His voice held a harsh contempt. "What every two-bit tough wants in Paydirt. The Holy Acre is crawling with them, from the soiled doves of the cribs to the hangers-on at Barraby's. Dave is no better. Only he came for higher stakes, that's all: a partnership in the Devil's Canyon Railroad!"

"Did he tell you this?"

"No!" Bill fished in his coat pocket for the crumpled envelope and handed it to her. "Dave dropped this in Doctor Kleeman's office yesterday."

She read the agreement Johnny Cruze had signed, then raised her gaze to him as she handed it back. "He must have known Johhny before he came here. What else does it prove?"

"I don't know," the sheriff answered. "But why did he pretend not to know Johnny when they met in my office? You were there, Laura. You saw it."

"I don't know why. But don't condemn him without knowing. Ask him! He'll tell you!"

"You seem almighty sure of that," he growled.

"He'll tell you," she repeated firmly. "He's that kind of a man."

Soltight jammed his hat on his head. "I'll ask him, if I ever see him again. He left town yesterday. Said he was going up to the mines. To see his partner, I reckon." He opened the door, then turned back to her.

"Forget him, girl!" His voice was harsh, demanding. "He's not for you. He'll be here for a while, and then he'll be gone —"

"Who is for me?" She came up, her eyes meeting his, dark with a sudden bitterness. "Who is for me?"

"Not Dave," he answered lamely. "A drifter — a gunman —"

"And Johnny Cruze?"

"No!" His voice was harsh now, definite.

"The man you've always admired, then — Sol Lengo?" She was punishing him now, her voice choked and hurting.

"I'll kill Sol first!" Soltight snarled. "Not Lengo!"

"Then who? Some miner from Big Lars? A worker from the stamp mills?"

"I don't know," he flung back at her. "I don't know. But not Dave Chance!" He turned and slammed the door in her face and went out into the dismal morning, feeling shaken and uncertain and angry at the world in general.

124

Laura's eyes were wet as she faced the closed door. It had come out at last, she thought numbly, the barrier her father had built around her; a barrier she had remained behind as long as she thought Rick and her father needed her.

But they didn't need her that way. Rick was a man, and her father had no right. He could hire himself a housekeeper. He had no right to chain her this way.

Rick's voice interrupted her. "You'll die an old maid, sis, if you listen to Father. Way he sees it, no man's good enough for you."

She turned. He was in the doorway, leaning against the framing. He looked so incongruous with his battered face, munching on a biscuit, that she had to smile.

"At least those bruises haven't interfered with your appetite," she observed. "Maybe you should go back to work."

His eyes grew serious. "I've been thinking of it." He flexed his fingers. "Gun hand's all right. I look worse than I feel. And I have some unfinished business across the river."

She became alarmed. "You wouldn't be foolish enough to pick another fight with Shane?"

His eyes held a mocking smile. "I learned my lesson there, sis. Packy's too much for me. But I don't intend to let that keep me from going across the river."

"But why ask for trouble?"

He took her firmly by the arm, led her to a kitchen chair and sat her down. "You've got a few things to

125

learn, sis. Now just wait a minute —" he interrupted her, holding a big palm in front of her face. "Let your kid brother talk for once. I've listened to you and Dad all my life. Now let me talk!"

She settled back, a doubtful smile on her face. Rick sat on a corner of the kitchen table and faced her, his bruised face more serious than she had ever seen it.

"I'm going across the river because if I don't, then it'll mean that the law isn't worth a tinker's dam in Paydirt. It'll mean that Duke won more than a fight that night in the Golden Nugget. It'll prove that he's forced Dad and me across the river. And if he can do that, one day he'll run us out of Paydirt altogether!"

"But that isn't your job or Dad's! It's Sol's job. He's the town marshal."

"So he is." Rick nodded. "But Sol represents his own kind of law — his own interests. I don't trust him. He and I never got along. But as long as I wear a deputy's badge, I've got as much right across the river as he has."

"The town council hired him!" she said, exasperated. "If Sol's that kind of man, that's what they hired! Why do you feel you have to interfere? Now you listen to me, Rick!" she said, rising from her chair and shaking a finger in his face. "It isn't only a matter of the law that is behind your wanting to cross the river. I know you — and I don't believe it."

"Maybe it's pride, too," he said angrily. "I got beaten, sis. I want to go back. I won't pick a fight with Packy. But I'm going back into the Golden Nugget

126

because I have a right to. And if you must hear me say it, I want to see Edith again."

She threw up her hands in a wry gesture of despair, and he came to her and put a big brotherly hand on her shoulder. "Now don't worry about me, sis. I'll be back before dinner. And I'll keep out of trouble."

She pulled away from him, ran into the living room and took the carbine from the glass-enclosed case under the elk's head. She held it on him as he came to the door.

"You're not going out at all, Rick!"

He laughed aloud, although it hurt his face. "You know, you look a lot better than that gun-toting female, Belle Star," he said proudly. "Saw her picture in the *Police Gazette* a while back. Practice a little, and you might even get to hit something with that gun."

Laura put the rifle down slowly and sat on the horsehair sofa. She felt suddenly old and uncared for, and she wept.

CHAPTER
FOURTEEN

The sheriff noticed the poster tacked to his office wall as he took out his key. He left the key in the lock and walked to it, a flush of anger darkening his face. Duke Mason's insolence stung.

The poster read:

GRUDGE FIGHT

PACKY SHANE issues a challenge to DAVE CHANCE, Sheriff's Deputy, to a pugilistic encounter to be held in a specially constructed arena in the empty lot behind the Golden Nugget. A $1000 purse will be awarded to the winner. Sheriff Bill Soltight is cordially invited to referee the match between protégé and Packy Shane.

Bill ripped the poster off his wall, tore it into several pieces and carried them inside, where he dumped them into his wastebasket. He tossed his hat on its hook and sat down to some correspondence on which he was behind. After a few minutes of empty-headed staring at the sheet of paper, pen in hand, he discarded the whole idea and went through yesterday's mail, which contained two new dodgers on men wanted in Cochise County.

128

But he was still too upset over Laura's bitter denunciation to bring himself to do the chores of his job. Duke's arrogance in forcing a showdown between the sheriff and himself rankled. He had little doubt that Duke had the town plastered with the posters, and he knew that the story of Dave's knockout of Packy had gotten around to every ear in Paydirt.

He stood his own bitter turmoil as long as he could; then he put on his hat and went out to the Café down the street. The poster stared at him from the back wall, issuing its blunt challenge, and Zig Artesi, the owner, came over to discuss the coming fight.

"Some folks figger it was a lucky punch," Zig ventured. "You think that big deputy of yours can take him?"

"I'd put my money on him," Soltight said, and he meant it. "But I don't think there's going to be any fight."

"Whole town's stirred up about it," Zig said. "Duke made it plain it's one side of the river against the other." Zig poured the sheriff's coffee. "Some of us lost a lot of money betting on Rick —"

"No one asked you to!" Soltight flared.

Zig flushed. "We ain't blaming you or Rick. All we ask is a chance to get back at Duke and his crowd. If this Dave Chance you hired is as good as you say —"

"I didn't say he was that good!" Soltight snapped. "Anyway, I don't pick fights for Dave. He gets paid as a deputy, not a fighter."

Zig backed away, his face turning sullen. "He'll have to fight," he muttered. "Packy won't let him stay in town until he does."

Soltight tossed a quarter on the counter. "Packy'll find himself in trouble if he comes looking for it," he said flatly. "I'm still the sheriff in Paydirt."

He went outside to find the sun spilling through a big break in the clouds. It warmed the street and cheered him somewhat. He felt angry but no longer confused, and examining himself, he decided that it was because he had backed his deputy in the argument in the Café. Laura was right, he reflected — a man should have a chance to do his own explaining.

He went back to his office and was working on the crude draft of his first report when Duke Mason entered. Packy was with him, a black turtle-necked sweater pulled over his thick chest.

Duke looked around the office, examining it with the curiosity of a man who sees it for the first time. Packy walked to the bulletin board and squinted at some of the old dodgers tacked to it.

Duke finally made his way to the desk and glanced into the wastebasket. "I see you read our poster," he said unpleasantly. His ear was taped. "What do you think of it, Sheriff?"

"I don't think of it at all!" Bill snarled. He swiveled around and jerked a thumb at Packy, who was fingering through the dodgers on the board. "Tell that bum of yours to keep his hands off government property!"

Packy turned on the balls of his feet and took a long stride toward the sheriff. Bill kicked his chair back and made a grab for his Colt.

130

Duke got between them. "Don't let him rile you, Packy!" he said sharply. "That's what he's looking for — an excuse to slap you in jail!"

Packy breathed hard through his teeth. "I don't want to hit him. I want that big deputy of his, Duke —"

"One thousand dollars," Duke said, turning to the sheriff. "Quite a piece of change for a drifter to make — if he beats Packy."

"Ask him, Duke." Bill's voice was cold. "I don't arrange his fights."

Duke frowned. "I will. I thought we'd find him here."

The sheriff shook his head. "He's gone up to Big Lars."

Duke was disappointed. "I plan to have the arena built by Saturday afternoon. When will he be back?"

"I don't know," Soltight said. "And maybe he won't want to fight."

Packy smacked his right fist into the palm of his left hand. "He'll fight, Sheriff, if I have to corner him in every doorway in town!"

Duke came to the desk and leaned on the palms of his hands. "Sheriff — he'll fight. He won't have a choice." His eyes mocked Soltight. "And you'll have a chance to win some of the money you lost betting on your boy."

Bill's jaw ridged. "Tell me more."

"It'll be a fair fight," Duke said. "You'll be the third man in the ring. Professional rules. A knockdown ends the round. You give a man five minutes to get up and continue the fight. The fight ends when one of the fighters can't get up."

Bill eyed the gambler with narrow distrust. "You must want this fight bad, Duke?"

Duke nodded. "I want to see him get what Rick got; only worse." He touched his bandaged ear. "Yeah, I want this fight bad, Sheriff."

Bill nodded. "I'll get Dave into that ring Saturday, but only on one condition."

"I'm listening."

"I want you out of Paydirt — you and your girls and your crew!" Bill leaned across the desk, breathing hard. "If Dave wins, you clear out. All of you!"

Duke sneered. "And if he loses?"

"I'll resign and leave town!"

Duke straightened, and his eyes clouded. He searched the proposition, suspecting it. He could find nothing tricky in it. He laughed thinly. "You think a lot of him, Sheriff. But your judgment in fighters is bad." He held out his hand. "It's a deal. Get Dave into that ring Saturday afternoon."

Packy walked to the desk as Duke turned away. He leaned over and flicked imaginary dirt from the sheriff's badge. "Better give it a last polish, Sheriff. You'll be turning it in after Saturday."

The canyon line train came down the mountain, its heavy pounding echoing in the gorge for a long time before its light poked through the darkness out of the canyon. The engineer whistled his approach warning. Black smoke billowed up, wreathed the tender and lay flat over the passenger car immediately behind. Two empty flat cars and a caboose completed the train.

Sheriff Soltight heard the train whistle as he came away from the livery stable. He had been looking for Sol Lengo since morning, after Duke and Shane had left his office.

The marshal wasn't in his cubbyhole office, and no one had seen him since yesterday. Doc Sonner, sweating out an attack of asthma in his back room, had mumbled something about the marshal riding out of town.

Lengo had sworn to kill Dave, and the knowledge that he had ridden out of town shortly after Dave's departure worried the sheriff. The marshal was a vengeful man, and if he had gone after Dave, the big deputy was in trouble.

Soltight fought a gnawing sense of helplessness. His break with Lengo had been sharp and sudden, but he still retained a grudging respect for the man's abilities.

Sol appeared, as if in answer to his thoughts. He came around the corner of Railroad Avenue and headed up the street toward the stables.

The sheriff waited for him. Sol rode past him, his dark face tight and inscrutable, and Bill, scowling, turned and followed him into the manure-littered yard.

"Did you find him?"

His question was blunt, and he was afraid of the answer. Sol lifted his left leg over his pommel and dropped lightly beside the tired animal. He turned slowly to face the sheriff.

"You worried, Bill?"

Bill checked the rise of his temper. Sol was evidently in an ugly mood, and he was most dangerous when he was quietest. And they were alone in the stable yard.

"You rode out after him, didn't you?"

Sol nodded bleakly.

"You find him?"

"If I had, he'd be across my saddle, head down," Sol said softly.

Bill breathed a sigh of relief. "Where'd you go?"

Sol turned and took a long stride toward him. It was late afternoon. The peaks shouldered out the sun, and a cool wind stirred the rubbish in the alley.

"Bill — I figure that's none of your business!"

A faint but definite warning chilled the older man. He and Sol had kept the law in Paydirt for more than six years, and this was the first break between them.

"There was a time when we worked together —" he began.

"That time's over," Sol cut in coldly. He had stopped and was watching Bill. "It ended the day you put a badge on that big gunslinger, Bill!"

"It didn't have to be that way," Bill Soltight muttered.

"A lot of things don't have to be," Sol sneered. "Right now you're in my way, old man!"

Bill's grip on his temper loosened. "Move me, Sol — move me!"

Sol took a slow step sideways. Then he turned all the way around and nodded slowly as the stableman's voice, coming out of the darkness of the stable, asked: "Want that animal rubbed down, Marshal?"

134

Soltight felt the naked tension seep slowly out of him as Sol, ignoring him now, led his cayuse up the ramp to the lanky hostler who was waiting. He felt suddenly drained, and he was surprised to find his hand shake as he reached for a cigar and lighted it.

He walked out to the street and turned toward the depot in time to see the train pull up by the platform. He watched it, hoping to see Dave step down out of the passenger car. But instead Johnny Cruze emerged, followed by several sullen-faced miners who immediately headed for the bridge and the fleshpots across the river.

Johnny had a few words with the station agent; then, spotting Bill on the corner, he came up the street toward him. He seemed worried.

"I just heard that Dave Chance took over Rick's job, Sheriff. You hired him?"

Bill nodded.

Johnny wet his lips. "I want to see him."

Soltight looked the dapper man over. "What about? His half of the Canyon line?"

It took Johnny by surprise. "Did Dave tell you?"

"In a way he did," Soltight said.

"Then he's a bigger fool than I suspected," Johnny said stiffly, and turned away.

Soltight laid a hand on his shoulder, jerked him around and grabbed a handful of lapel. He pulled Johnny up close.

"Just what sort of game are you playing, Cruze? Did you send for that big feller? Or is he just another sucker you're planning to double-cross as soon as he's served his purpose?"

Johnny reddened. "I don't see that it's any of your business, Sheriff!"

Bill shook him. "Like fun it isn't! You've been shooting off your mouth about the way I've been doing my job ever since Ed Minik and Ramsey disappeared with the Lucky Cuss payroll. You've hinted I've turned blind to the troubles you've been having with the railroad. But whether you like it or not, I'm still sheriff here. And if you've gone and hired yourself a trouble-shooter, I want to know about it!"

Johnny looked around. He was pulled up on his toes, and the sheriff's big fist was bunched under his chin; the humiliation showed in Johnny's eyes.

A half-dozen people had stopped, listening to them. Several others were crossing the street toward them.

Johnny squirmed free and smoothed down his coat front. "I ought to tell you to go shoot yourself!" he said blankly. "But I'll tell you about Dave. In your office, Sheriff. Not here."

Soltight nodded grimly. "Maybe you'd better."

They walked to the law office. Sheriff Soltight closed the door and walked to his desk and pulled out his top drawer. He tossed Dave's envelope to Johnny Cruze.

"You've seen this before," he stated harshly. "An agreement, signed by you, making Dave Chance your partner in the Devil's Canyon Railroad."

Johnny was puzzled and angry. "Dave give this to you?"

"He dropped it inside Doctor Kleeman's office," Soltight answered. "He ran into some trouble in Barraby's, trying to locate one of the two men who

136

killed Ramsey. Picked up some birdshot, and Doc Kleeman cut it out of him."

"Oh!" Johnny made a gesture with his hands. "I didn't think Dave would tell you."

"Why not?"

"Because this was between us, a business deal. I owed him that much —"

Soltight took a turn around his desk and came up to Johnny, who flinched and took a step backward. "I don't trust you as far as that door," the sheriff grated. "I want to hear what there is between you and Dave. I know why you cut me in on the railroad, in the beginning. But Dave —"

"I'm sorry about that, Sheriff —"

"Sit down and shut up!" Bill snarled. "You never were sorry about anything in your life!"

Johnny whitened. "I don't have to stay here and listen to that kind of irresponsible talk!"

Soltight cut Johnny off at the door. "You'll stay long enough to listen to what I have to say. You took me in as a partner because you expected trouble. You needed someone to risk his neck to keep the railroad going — you didn't want to risk yours. As sheriff, it would be my job to do the worrying for both of us!"

"It's still your job, regardless of whether you own part of the railroad or not!" Johnny snapped. "I offered you an interest in the line because I wanted to do you a favor. I knew you felt Severson and Fillmore had put you out of business — and I didn't want to buck a sheriff with a grudge against the railroad when I took it over. And there was another consideration —"

"Leave Laura out of this conversation," the sheriff interrupted. He jabbed a forefinger against Johnny's shirt. "Let's get back to Dave Chance. Who is he? How does he rate a partnership with you?"

Johnny took a long breath. "It's a long story, Sheriff. You want to listen to all of it?"

"I've got plenty of time," Soltight rasped. "And there's whiskey in my desk, in case you run a little dry telling it."

Johnny told him. It took the better part of an hour to do it, and by that time it had turned dark outside. They stood in the gloom of the office, Bill slumped back in his chair, while Johnny moved about restlessly.

"An ex-pug," Bill said. "I took him for some gunslinger you had sent for."

"Dave is a fair hand with a gun; nothing more," Johnny said. "But he was a great fighter. I —"

"You ran out on him?" Bill looked curiously at Johnny. "Why?"

Johnny shoved his hands deep into his pockets and teetered on his toes. He looked small and dapper, but, for the first time since Bill had known him, a little flustered and uncertain.

"I liked him. Believe that. But I was tired of camp fights, of living in cheap hotels, of small purses. And Dave was taking a lot of punishment. I didn't want to see him take any more."

Soltight shook his head. "You didn't do it for him, Johnny!"

138

Johnny shrugged. "That was part of it. The big reason I left Montana was twenty thousand dollars. Our end of the purse, plus what I had bet on Dave. For the first time since Dave and I were together, I had enough money to take a big gamble —"

"And you left Dave holding the bag?" Soltight came to his feet, a thick shadow against the wall. "No wonder he came after your hide!"

"Dave was a cautious man," Johnny said defensively. "He would never have let me gamble with that money. If I had stuck by him, we'd be broke by this time."

"What does he have now?"

"He wanted ten thousand," Johnny answered. "I gave him half the railroad instead."

"A poor bargain." The sheriff moved against the windows, turning to face Johnny. "You're about to go broke. If the Lucky Cuss shuts down, so will the other mines on Big Lars. And without freight to haul, the railroad will go broke, just the way it happened to Fillmore and Severson." He paused, and the silence extended between them.

"And what does Dave Chance get out of that, Cruze?"

"It's a gamble," Johnny admitted. "But the purse is the biggest one he'll ever fight for!"

"With him risking everything," Soltight said grimly. He shook his head. "I was smart enough to back out of our deal. Now Dave's in the same spot. To get anything out of the business deal he made, he has to save your neck — and risk his. And it's possible he already has lost his gamble."

"What do you mean?"

Soltight jabbed a finger toward the window. "Dave left yesterday to ride up to Big Lars. He wanted to see you. Did he get there?"

Johnny shook his head. "He didn't come to the Lucky Cuss."

"Then he didn't make it!" Soltight reached for his hat. "I've been a darn fool for a long time. But it's time I began wearing spectacles."

"Where are you going?"

"Nowhere, tonight. But tomorrow you and I are going up the canyon to the Roost, in your private car, Cruze. And if I don't get the right answers from Holly Jackson, I'm coming back to ask them of Sol Lengo."

Johnny wet his lips nervously. "Sol mixed up in this?"

Bill nodded. He walked to the door, turned. "The Santa Fe came in yesterday. There's a sealed package in the railroad safe for you; I've put a special guard over it. I think it's your payroll."

"Thanks," Johnny said. His voice was stiff.

"The guard's wages are charged to you," Bill said. "I don't give a hoot what happens to it, once you take charge of it. But let me give you some advice. Let that money stay there until we get back from the Roost!"

"I'm taking the payroll up to the mine myself," Johnny said. "But I'll wait, Sheriff . . ."

CHAPTER
FIFTEEN

Dave had hit the water hard, on the back of his shoulders. He felt a wrench in his neck, and then he lost contact with reality and was only vaguely aware, as if in a dream, of being submerged and spewed up again. He coughed water out of his throat and made a weak effort to guide himself. He hit a rock. He felt the pain in his left thigh, and it shocked him back to an awareness of his plight. Instinctively he reached out for a handhold. His fingers closed over a jagged edge of slick rock, and he held on grimly while the current tried to take him away, frothing against his side.

He and the dog had parted upon impact. He didn't see the animal again, but the burning in his shoulder, close to the base of his neck, reminded him of the animal's teeth.

When he regained enough strength, he looked up. The rain came down hard on his face, and the night blotted out the Roost. The rushing water absorbed any other sound.

He looked about him. He could see only the froth of the stream farther on, gleaming faintly, like a white phosphorescence, and the sound of its passage filled the gorge with a hollow booming. The water was cold, chilling him to the bone. He felt the strength seeping out of him, and he reached up desperately, seeking escape. But his groping fingers encountered only slick rock above him.

He would have to take his chances and ride the strong current downstream. He couldn't hang on much longer.

Dave pushed himself away from the rock and immediately felt the force of the water take him, pull him around and hurry him on. He tried to guide himself, pushing away from snags in his path. He went down a raceway with only minor bruising encounters with underwater obstacles, and then the waters stilled again and he treaded water, searching the darkness for an avenue of escape. A faint strip of white drew him toward the north wall.

He found himself climbing out of the water onto a small pebbly beach, less than six feet deep. Behind him a dark sheer wall blotted out the sky. He crouched on the rocks, breathing in shallow gulps. He was out of the water, but he was as effectively trapped as though he had wandered into a cage and shut the door behind him. As far as he could make out, he was in a deep gorge hemmed in by sheer cliffs, and he might have to travel for miles before he could stumble on a way out of it.

The rain pelted him. He crawled back against the cliff, and the wall partially protected him. He shivered violently. He was more cold than hurt; probing at the base of his neck, he decided that the lacerations from the dog's teeth had done little beyond breaking through

142

the skin. His more probable danger from the bite would be the risk of infection.

The more obvious aspects of his predicament knotted his stomach. He knew if he remained there through the night, he'd be a sitting duck for Lengo and Holly in the morning. And he was sure they'd be looking for him, from the rim of the gorge, to satisfy themselves that he was dead.

But he waited the night out, having no choice. Beyond the small beach, the stream rushed through a narrow mill-race, and he could hear the booming of what might be a small falls beyond.

With the gray smudge of dawn, the rain slackened. The dark canyon walls came out of the deep night, rising gray and dismal above him.

He stood at the water's edge and searched the gorge. A gray mist clung like a protective wall over the stream. But there was enough daylight now for Dave to see the narrow ledge that ran along the opposite wall.

Grimly he made his decision. There was only one way to get out of there, and that meant going back the way he had come!

He waited, crouched in a narrow crack in the cliff until the light strengthened. The sun came out for a few moments, painting the top of the gorge with wet brilliance, then disappeared.

The heavy pounding was, at first, only an undertone to the rushing stream. But it grew louder, its hammer strokes reverberating in the hills. Dave's teeth gritted. The train from Big Lars!

Hope rose up and choked him with its aftermath of despair. He couldn't make it in time; at best, all he could hope for was that the coming of the train would interrupt the search for him.

He'd have to take the plunge now. His cold, aching body shrank from it, but his iron will shoved him into the water. He crossed the comparatively quiet pool to the ledge on the other side and pulled himself out, shivering. Then he crawled along it, working back toward the spot where he had fallen.

Twice the ledge broke off, and he had to fight the current to make it to the next section. But eventually he reached the deeper pool under the overhanging balcony from which he had tumbled. The rope was there, pulled taut by the oaken bucket submerged in the pool.

Close by, the Mallet engine whistled hoarsely, signaling its approach to the watering station. Dave didn't know if it would stop, but he knew this would be the most likely time to make an attempt to get out of the gorge.

He took a deep breath, dove into the pool and fought the slow current until his fingers closed around the thick rope. Then he clung, gathering his strength.

It was close to forty feet straight up to the balcony. He wrapped the rope around his right forearm and pulled himself up slowly. The first six feet took the most out of him. The ache reached deep into his gut. But once out of the water, he could use his legs, wrapping the rope around them to hold him, easing the steady strain on his arms and shoulders.

144

He went up slowly, blindly, doggedly, not allowing himself to think of the possibility that Holly Jackson or Sol Lengo might be waiting for him. He made it to the balcony just as the train curved past the clearing, out of sight of the balcony. He heard its hoarse whistle of greeting, but it didn't stop.

Dave swung over the railing and crouched by the door, getting his breath back in slow, laboring gulps. The rain clouds had moved on, pushed westward by a rising wind.

He reached for his Remington. Miraculously, it was still in his holster; this became more understandable when he tried to draw it. It was jammed in deep, its front sight caught in a crack in the leather. He had no clear idea how it had gotten there — he knew he had had it in his hand when he had gone over the balcony.

Some things a man does through habit — that was the only explanation he could give of the incident.

At any rate, he had the Remington in his hand now as he cautiously swung the door open and stepped quickly into the long room beyond.

There was no one in sight. The blaze in the fireplace drew Dave immediately. He stripped off his wet clothing and stood in his underwear, his back so close to the fire it started his long-johns steaming.

The remain of breakfast were still on the long table where he and Holly had eaten supper the night before. There was no sound from the kitchen, but he went to it to make sure.

The house was momentarily deserted. Outside, the laboring of the Mallet engine was fading. He went to

145

the lone window which faced the clearing and saw Holly, shotgun dangling carelessly by his side, coming up the path to the house.

Dave pulled back to one side of the door and waited for him.

Holly Jackson was a worried man. He had made a perfunctory search of the gorge after Lengo had gone. But the rain and the clinging mist had discouraged him. Still, he had walked to the point where the stream dropped twenty feet into Devil's Creek and had stood there, eyeing the boiling water. He had seen nothing of Dave Chance or of Jake, his dog — he had little hope of seeing either one again.

He had come back when he had heard the train. Waiting by the tower, he had waved to the engineer as he usually did. He saw Johnny Cruze through the window of the passenger car and waved to him, but Johnny seemed preoccupied and made no gesture of recognition.

Sol had left several hours ago, but Holly knew that the train would probably beat the marshal into Paydirt.

He turned away then and walked back to the house. He still had to bury Manny, and he didn't relish the job. Getting rid of the two horses had more appeal. He knew of a small valley in the hills where he could turn them loose until he came for them again.

And he decided that he would return for them soon. The game was getting too risky. He wasn't going to wait for the next payroll, considering what he had been paid for his work. It was nowhere near enough.

146

But if the sheriff found out — ? He caressed his scrawny neck with long fingers, not liking the implications of this.

He opened the door, and the man who appeared in front of him in long underwear and holding a cocked gun was a nightmare to which he couldn't immediately adjust. He stood with open mouth, his shotgun pointed at the floor, his lanky body running stiffly together like long unoiled machinery.

"Get inside and shut the door!" Dave snapped.

Holly kicked the door shut.

"Put that gun on the table, slow and easy! Now move away from it!"

Holly obeyed. He turned and walked toward the far wall, his Adam's apple bobbing nervously.

"Where's the marshal?"

Holly made a limp gesture in the direction of the door.

"He rode back to town about three hours ago."

"Where's Manny?"

"He — he's dead. His body's out in the shed."

Dave considered this. "You knew Manny," he said grimly. "And it was the marshal in the kitchen with you last night. They came up here to kill me."

"I didn't know," Holly blurted hoarsely, "what Sol was up to. I swear it, mister. He came into the kitchen while I was getting Manny some of the rabbit stew."

"He's been here before," Dave cut him off. "So has Manny. This is where Irving Ramsey was dumped off the train, isn't it?"

Holly tried to bluff it out, but he didn't have the guts for it. "Ramsey? I don't know what you're talking about —"

"You know exactly what I'm saying!" Dave snarled. He walked up close to Holly, and the gaunt caretaker shrank from the threatening gun muzzle. "You told me yourself that the trail is worse from here on up to Big Lars. Ramsey couldn't have been dumped off any place below here. So it had to be here, where there was someone waiting to get him out of sight in a hurry."

Holly stared mutely at the muzzle of Dave's gun.

"Ramsey was chloroformed and rolled off the platform," Dave told him harshly. "You picked him up and lugged him into the house, and later took him through the hills to some hide out where Zack Miller and Voss were waiting."

Holly's resistance collapsed. "How did you know, mister?"

"I know that much. I know Doc Sonner was the man who chloroformed Ramsey and Ed Minik. What I don't know, and what you're going to tell me, is who kept the money. Doc Sonner?"

Holly caved in. "I ain't gonna hang for nobody, mister. Sure, I took Ramsey and Ed Minik, before him, to the shack on the other side of the hills. But I had nothing to do with killing them. I was in the middle, mister. I had to play along with the marshal and Doc Sonner, or I wouldn't have lasted here ten minutes."

"You'll testify to that before a circuit judge?"

Holly licked his lips. "I'll testify. But if you take me down to Paydirt, I won't stay alive for any trial."

148

"We'll chance that," Dave said thinly. The warmth felt good against his back; it seemed to soak up the aches and pains of his bruises. "We'll have some more of that rabbit stew while my clothes dry. Then we'll ride down to Paydirt together . . ."

Sheriff Soltight was in Mike's Bar when his son Rick came in. Bill was sitting in a four-handed game of draw poker and losing money. His mind wasn't on the cards, but he had to kill time, and he was too restless to sleep.

Rick walked up to the bar, asked for a glass of beer and grinned at the scowl on his father's face. Despite his bruises, he looked cheerful.

"Laura wants to see you," he said casually.

"What are you doing out of the house?" Bill countered angrily.

"Getting some night air," Rick said. "Doc says it's good for me. Less germs floating around at night —"

"But more darn fools," his father snapped. "Go on home, and tell Laura I'll be there in ten minutes."

"She wants you right away," Rick interrupted. "You know how Laura is when she sets her mind on something."

Soltight pushed his hand into the discards. "Must be important," he muttered, and followed Rick outside.

His son didn't go home. He turned down the side street and then cut back through an alley which brought them out to Gold Street again, a block from the sheriff's office. Soltight followed him. They turned quickly down the narrow alley separating the office building from the darkened structure next to it. Rick went to the side door and knocked twice, sharply.

The sheriff growled: "What kind of feedaddle you up to, boy?"

The door opened. A tall figure loomed up in the dim light which flickered inside the office. Dave's voice was quick and sharp. "Come in and shut the door!"

Bill walked in, surprised and puzzled. His son closed the door and bolted it. He looked at the dim light and beyond it to the drawn shades. The door to the cell block was open; he heard a man move back there.

He looked at Dave. "I thought you were dead," he said. "I planned to ride up the Canyon trail in the morning —"

"I saved you the trouble," Dave answered shortly. "Where's Sol Lengo?"

"Across the river, where he usually hangs out."

Dave was relieved. "Gives me a breather," he muttered. "I need a good night's sleep."

"Sol rode up the Canyon trail after you," the sheriff probed. "He came back this afternoon and said he hadn't seen you. What happened?"

Dave told him. "We left Manny in the woodshed. Jackson's in a cell in back. He'll testify at the trial, if we keep him alive that long."

"He'll be in one piece," Rick growled. "I'll sleep in here myself until the judge gets to town, if I have to."

Soltight sank slowly into a chair. "Doc Sonner. No." He shook his head. "Dave — not Sonner. He and I —"

"Talk to Holly yourself," Dave said.

Bill made a weary gesture. "Later." He looked up at the big man he had hired. "What are you planning to do about Sol?"

"Get a good night's rest first," Dave replied. "I'll see the marshal in the morning."

"He's too fast for you," Bill said heavily.

"I have no choice."

The sheriff got to his feet. "You could get on a fresh horse and be halfway to Concho by morning."

"I've got business in town," Dave said. His tone was final.

Bill snorted softly. "A half-interest in Johnny Cruze's railroad?"

"So Doctor Kleeman gave you my envelope?" Dave smiled faintly. "I would have told you, before I rode out yesterday. I decided not to take it, Sheriff. I'll settle with Johnny Cruze for five thousand dollars.' "

Soltight eyed him with new interest. "It sounds like a bad bargain. But knowing Johnny Cruze, I think it's wiser — if you can get the money from him."

"I'll get it."

"He owes you more," Bill pointed out. "He left you stranded in Montana without a cent, while he had twenty thousand dollars from that last fight you had. Yeah, I know all about it," he said, putting up a hand to forestall Dave's questions. "Collared Johnny this afternoon, right after he came to town. He told me about you."

"I wouldn't believe half of it," Dave said dryly.

Bill looked him up and down. "You think a night's rest will help?"

"Depends what it's supposed to do," Dave said.

Bill walked to his desk and brought out one of Duke's posters. He handed it to Dave.

"Everybody on this side of the river has bet money on you. Think you can take him?"

Dave shook his head. "I quit fighting two years ago, Bill."

Rick said softly: "That's one fight I'd like to see, Dave."

Dave said shortly: "No."

"They've got these posted all over town. Packy's been talking in every bar on both sides of the river. He'll be after you, Dave. You'll have to fight — or quit town!"

"No!"

Bill sighed. "I didn't want to tell you this. But I made a bet with Duke. If you beat Packy, he quits town with the whole kit and caboodle of them!"

"And if Packy wins?" Dave's voice was grim.

Bill shrugged. "I'll resign and move out of Paydirt."

Dave threw up his hands. "That was a fool bet, Bill. Packy's a tough hombre. And I haven't had a fight in two years."

"I made the bet," Bill said heavily. "I promised Duke you'd be in that ring Saturday." He tossed the poster into a corner. "It was a fool bet," he agreed. "I wasn't thinking of you, Dave. I was thinking of Duke, and how bad I wanted him out of town."

Dave massaged his knuckles. "Sol comes first," he said quietly. "We'll talk about Packy later."

152

CHAPTER
SIXTEEN

Saturday morning dawned cool and clear.

Doc Sonner came out of his office, looking pale and drawn. He crossed the street and went into the hotel for breakfast as was his custom. It was the only meal he ate at the hotel.

He was drinking his second cup of coffee when he saw Dave enter the dining room. He wasn't wearing his glasses, but now he took them out of their case, which he kept in his breast pocket, and put them on. The lenses covered the dismay in his eyes.

Dave looked over the diners and spotted him. He came over to join the doctor, limping slightly. He smiled.

"Mind if I join you?"

Doc Sonner shook his head and waved to a chair across from him.

Dave sat down, caught the eye of a waitress and gave her his order.

"You've got a healthy appetite," Doc said admiringly. He had recovered his composure. "At this hour I can't stand more than biscuits and coffee."

"You need to get outside more," Dave suggested.

"I need to go back twenty years," Doc said. He smiled and reached in his vest pocket for a thin black cigar. "Bill told me you rode up to Big Lars. Still looking for someone, Dave?"

"Found him," Dave said.

Sonner cupped his match and brought it to his cigar. The smoke puffed up, hiding his eyes.

"Hope you've run down something on those payroll robberies," he said. "Bill hasn't been too popular lately, and they haven't helped him any."

Dave looked up as the waitress brought him his order. He took a sip of his coffee, then leaned back. "Ramsey didn't run off with the payroll," he said casually. "Neither did Ed Minik."

Sonner's smile was cold. "I never believed they did, either."

"No, you didn't," Dave agreed. "It puzzled me at first. Bill was sure they had. And you were Bill's friend."

"You've used the wrong tense," Sonner said. His voice had grown thin. "I still am Bill's friend. But I manage to do my own thinking."

"I'm sure of it," Dave answered.

The doctor pushed his empty cup and saucer aside and reached inside his coat pocket for change. He placed a quarter beside the cup.

Dave said pleasantly, "Don't go yet, Mr. Sonner. Have another cup of coffee."

"I've had two. That's my limit."

"Stay anyway." Dave's request was an order.

Sonner's eyes flashed angrily. "Aren't you taking that badge Bill gave you a little too seriously?"

"Quite seriously," Dave agreed. "So seriously that I'm ordering you to stay here until I finish breakfast."

Sonner started to get up, his face flushing. "Now see here —"

Dave's right hand came up from below the table, and the Remington's snout rested on the tablecloth. "Sit down, Doc. This *is* an order!"

Sonner sat down, his face paling. "This is the most high-handed exhibition I've ever been subjected to," he gritted. "When I see Bill —"

"You'll see the sheriff shortly," Dave cut him off. "He'll have a few things to say to you."

"You sound like a dime novel!" Sonner said contemptuously. "I'll wait for Bill."

"Thanks." Dave's voice was dry. "Sure you don't want another cup of coffee?"

Sonner declined coldly. "Just why are you keeping me?"

"Holly Jackson talked," Dave said. He finished chewing on a piece of ham and added: "He's in jail right now, with Bill keeping an eye on him. He'll keep talking, Doc, at the trial."

Sonner's bold front collapsed. "Holly's in jail?"

"He's been there all night. I brought him in."

The doctor's thin hand shook as he knocked ash from his cigar. "All right, Dave," He made a slight gesture of defeat. "I told Sol you'd be a hard man to beat." He gestured to the waitress. "I'll take that cup of coffee now."

Dave slid the Remington back into his holster and finished his coffee. The dining room grew crowded. It was nine o'clock when the sheriff appeared in the archway leading to the lobby. He looked over the room, caught Dave's eyes and nodded.

Doc Sonner saw him and started to rise. He made a gesture to Soltight, but the sheriff ignored him. He turned and disappeared into the lobby.

Sonner turned to Dave. His voice was curious. "What now?"

Dave called for his check, paid it, left a tip. "We're leaving," he told Sonner.

"Where are we going?"

"To your place. To pick up the money."

"Money? You don't think —" Sonner started to laugh. "I'm not that much of a fool, Dave."

"Neither Ramsey nor Ed Minik had the money with them when you dropped them off at the Roost," Dave said. "You had it. You still do."

"Holly tell you that?"

Dave nodded.

Sonner shrugged. "Let's go."

They left together, like old friends. But Dave walked slightly behind the small thin man. They turned into Gold Street and headed for Doctor Sonner's office.

Before they got to Sonner's office, Sol Lengo came around the corner from the direction of the bridge. The marshal was walking fast, as though he were hurrying some place. When he saw Dave and Doctor Sonner, he stopped.

156

He was about fifty feet away and across Gold Street. He stood on the windy corner, a lean, deadly man, suddenly bent on killing.

Two men coming up the walk suddenly caught the meaning of the scene and ducked abruptly into a doorway. Doc Sonner stepped away from Dave and flattened himself against the side of the building.

"You won't make it," he whispered to Dave.

Dave waited. The Remington was in its holster, close to his fingers. The wind ran up the street, swirling a piece of old newspaper around in a giddy circle. Dave felt like a man on the edge of a precipice, looking down into a deep dark hole . . .

"I'm coming for you," the marshal said. His voice rang cold and clear. "I'll start shooting when I get to the middle of the street."

Dave had no answer for him.

Lengo stepped off the walk. Bill Soltight stepped into view on the same side of the street. He came out of a doorway less than twenty feet behind the marshal. His voice cut like the crack of a whip across the windy silence.

"Don't do it, Sol!"

Sol pulled up with the quick easy grace of a hunting cat surprised by some movement behind him. He didn't look at Bill.

"Keep out of this, Sheriff!"

"No!"

Sol's voice thinned. *"Keep out of it, Bill!"*

"Holly talked!" Soltight's voice was harsh, desperate. "It won't work now, Sol. Dave's my deputy."

Sol wavered for just an instant. His yellowish gaze flickered over Doc Sonner, cowering against the building behind Dave.

"I'm going to kill him!" he said. His voice was brittle, unyielding. "Don't make me take you, too, Bill!"

Soltight's face was that of a man condemned. He had worked with Sol Lengo for six years, and habit had worn a deep groove in him.

"Sol, don't be a fool. If you kill Dave, you'll hang —"

The marshal turned and fired just as a puff of dust flickered across his vision. Bill's Colt went off a split-second later, the bullet missing his toes by a half-inch and tearing a jagged hole in the plank walk. He staggered and fell against the building and slowly slid down.

Sol pivoted and almost got to Dave, despite this interruption. He fired too quickly. His bullet grazed Doc Sonner, who sank to the walk, his face drained bloodless.

Dave's bullets hit home. The marshal jerked like a stuffed doll being jabbed with a blunt stick. He fell hard, rolled over and twitched a little before he died.

Dave ran across the street to Bill Soltight. The sheriff was sitting up, his face showing the shock of the bullet in his shoulder. Bu he still held his Colt in his hand.

"I'm all right," he grated. "Get Doc Sonner. Don't let him get away."

Dave turned. Sonner was still on his hands and knees by the building. He seemed to be praying.

"He'll keep," Dave said. "I'll send someone for Doctor Kleeman."

158

"No." Bill's voice was tired. "Doc Sonner will do. He's worked on me since we came to Paydirt, fifteen years ago. Don't want to change now."

Dave shrugged. "I'll get him for you, Bill."

CHAPTER
SEVENTEEN

The crowd began collecting around the makeshift ring set up in the back lot behind the Golden Nugget shortly after noon.

Johnny Cruze appeared a little later. He circulated around the various saloons, and by two o'clock he had bet ten thousand dollars on Dave Chance.

By two-thirty he began to get worried. The crowd grew restless. Some commented angrily: "I thought there was gonna be a fight . . ." A sullen murmur of disappointment went up from the waiting men.

The sound carried across the river, reaching through the sheriff's open window. He was propped up on his pillow, his face pale and somewhat drawn with pain.

Dave was in the room with him. Laura and Rick had left them alone and were waiting in the kitchen.

"I have to go, Bill," Dave said. "It's either get it over with now — or start running." He gave a small shrug of his shoulders. "I don't want to run."

The sheriff licked dry lips. "I agreed to the fight, Dave. I had no right doing this to you, putting you on the spot. I don't want you to go out there, feeling that I forced you into it."

"No one forces me into anything," Dave said. "But I owe you something for this morning. It'll be a pleasure taking it out on Packy Shane!"

Soltight sighed. "Win or lose, Dave," he said, holding out his hand, "good luck."

Dave, grinning, took it briefly.

Laura stopped him at the door. "Is this the way it has to be, Dave?"

He nodded.

"I'll be waiting," she said simply. "With coffee — the way you like it."

He studied her, reading the deeper message in her eyes. "I'll be back in fifteen minutes," he promised.

He turned to Rick. "I want a half-dozen men you can trust, with rifles."

Rick's bruised face creased in a wide grin. "I know just the men you want," he said happily.

"I'll wait for you at the bridge," Dave said. "I'll tell you what I want there . . ."

Duke Mason had erected a makeshift ring for the occasion. It had a rough plank deck about fifteen feet square and was bounded by two sagging rope strands. The time-keeper was an old man with a stovepipe hat balanced on a shiny bald head. He sat on a stool with a bell on a packing case in front of him and a small hammer and a gold watch beside it.

He took his job seriously.

A cry went up from the restless crowd as Dave and Rick appeared. Duke and Packy Shane were already at ringside. Packy was sitting morosely in his corner, a purple robe across his wide shoulders. He didn't get up as Dave and Rick climbed through the ropes, but he grinned wickedly and sat up straighter, saying something out of the side of his mouth to Duke.

Rick walked over to Mason. "I'm taking my father's place in the ring," he said. "Any objections?"

Duke shook his head. Packy looked at him, sneering. "Just don't get in my way, kid!"

Rick glanced at Packy's taped fists. "What's that for?"

"Rules," Duke said thinly. "Doctor Kleeman will see that your fighter's hands get the same treatment."

Rick turned. Doctor Kleeman was already in Dave's corner, winding gauze over Dave's knuckles. He walked back and saw that Johnny Cruze was behind Dave, holding Dave's coat and shirt.

Doctor Kleeman finished taping Dave's hands, glanced at Duke and nodded. He ducked under the top strand and left the ring.

Duke left Packy's corner, walked to the center of the ring and held up his hands to quiet the crowd.

"Gentlemen: This bout will be conducted according to the Queensbury rules. There will be no kicking or gouging, no biting. When a man is knocked down, the round ends. He'll have five minutes to get up and resume fighting. When a fighter is no longer able to continue, the bout ends."

He looked to Dave's corner. "Agreed?"

Dave nodded. Rick shrugged.

Duke made a come-together motion with his hands. "When you're ready —"

162

A strange disturbance rumbled through the crowd. Men began turning, looking up at the encircling roof tops.

Duke stiffened. Six men were posted on the roofs overlooking the back lot. They all held rifles.

He turned to Rick Soltight. "What's that for?"

"Insurance."

Duke paled. "I said this would be a fair fight."

"We believe you," Rick answered. "The boys just decided they wanted box seats."

Duke bit his lips. The crowd grew impatient. Someone yelled: "Start the fight, Duke! Start the fight . . ."

Rick jerked a thumb toward the ropes. "Get out of the ring, Duke."

He waited until the gambler had left, then gave the signal to the old man in the stovepipe hat. The bell rang.

It was a bloody, brutal fight. It opened fast, with Packy coming three quarters of the way across the small ring to get his sneer smeared in red across his face. He went back on his heels, and Dave's right-hand smash under his heart dropped him.

The bell rang, and the sound was lost in the roar of the crowd.

Packy turned over slowly and painfully got to his feet. Nate, his second, came out of his corner and helped Shane to his stool.

The confidence had been shocked out of the Golden Nugget fighter. He sprawled limply on his stool, sucking in painful breaths while Nate daubed blood away from his smashed lips.

Duke had an unlighted cigar between his teeth. He stood by the ringside, shaken and uncertain.

The bell rang.

Packy came out cautiously now. Dave limped to meet him. He feinted twice, missed with a wild left hook, and Packy split the skin over his left eye. Dave put his face against Packy's shoulder and drove his hands into the man's mid-section. Packy grunted and pulled away and chopped twice at Dave's neck.

Dave went in again, knowing he had to end this fast. He didn't have the stamina for a grueling fight, or the timing.

Packy played it safe, but opened up once, and Dave tagged him with a looping right that dropped him.

Packy wasn't hurt. He walked unaided to his corner, and Duke whispered harshly in his ears: "Take these and finish him!"

Packy spit blood into the spittoon and covered himself as he took the two small lead cylinders from Duke. They fitted snugly in the palms of his hands . . .

The bell rang.

Dave moved out and ran into a blow to the mid-section that doubled him up. Packy's fist exploded behind his right ear. He went down with a great roaring in his head . . .

Rick's anxious face floated out of the gray mist, wavered, finally came back to size. Dave found himself propped up on his stool, with Rick hovering over him.

164

"Four minutes," Rick whispered hoarsely. "I thought you'd never come out of it."

Dave's grin was an imprint on his face.

"Ready?" Rick whispered.

Dave nodded. He knew what Packy had in his fists. But if he tried to call attention to them, it might end up in a free-for-all, spreading out to the partisan crowd around the ring.

The bell rang.

Packy came out to meet him more confidently. Dave's knees wobbled slightly as he waited. It was an old trick, but Packy fell for it. He whipped a hard right to Dave's face which Dave only partially avoided. Dave staggered. Packy dropped his guard and came in, ready to end it.

Dave fell back against the ropes and bounced up, and Packy ran into Dave's right hand. His eyes crossed and his knees buckled. Dave smashed at his unprotected stomach, back at Packy's jaw, and then struck a one-two smash into Packy's face as he began to crumble.

The Golden Nugget fighter hit the rough board flooring with his face. He bounced a little from the impact. He didn't move.

Nate and Duke came in to get their fighter. Dave picked up the lead cylinders which had skidded out of Packy's hands. He tossed them to Rick.

"Get him up!" he told Duke. "Throw water on him!"

Packy stirred weakly at the end of three minutes. Just before the five-minute bell, Duke shoved him into the ring.

165

Packy shuffled forward, his face a bloody mess, and peered at Dave. Dave hit him twice. Shane went back against the ropes and toppled over them. He didn't get up . . .

Laura stood on the porch facing the small gate and listened to the sounds from across the river. There was fear in her, similar to the fear she had felt when Rick had fought Packy Shane. Every wild surge of sound from the crowd was like a knife thrusting into her.

Behind her, in the bedroom, she knew her father, too, was listening. Silence fell abruptly. She strained then, looking down the road to the corner around which they would come.

She seemed to wait an eternity.

Then Rick and Dave appeared. Rick broke away and began to run toward her, and from the look on his face she knew what had happened. He came to her, and although she laughed there were tears in her eyes.

He said: "Packy didn't have a chance, sis," and went inside to tell his father.

Dave limped through the gate. He was carrying his coat over his shoulder, and his face was battered. But his eyes were clear.

He waited at the foot of the stairs.

Laura said: "Come inside, Dave. I have your coffee waiting."

He went up the steps then and took her into his arms and kissed her.